Wrath Of A Sidepiece

Author Tray Real

Published by Author Tray Real, 2023.

The Wrath
Of A
Sidepiece

This is a work of fiction. Similarities to real people, places, or events are entirely coincidental.

WRATH OF A SIDEPIECE

First edition. November 8, 2023.

Copyright © 2023 Author Tray Real.

ISBN: 979-8223781073

Written by Author Tray Real.

Prologue

"Get the hell out of my house and do not, I repeat, DO NOT bring your cheating thieving ass around here ever again! Women like you deserve a snake, not a dog. A dog would be too loyal for you! I have never, in all my life, met a woman so scandalous!"

I began launching articles of clothing, make-up, a few wigs, and her funky ass shoes out my front door. It's pretty messed up when you're confronted with the truth and have to actually think about how the power of a woman's beauty, and her vagina, can make you forget that you have morals and self-respect. I became someone I didn't recognize, chasing after a gold-digging user. I saw the signs, yet I shook them off. What she offered on her physical level superseded my common sense. I began looking forward to having sex versus getting to know her on a mental level. I would have known she couldn't build a table, let alone sit at one, if I would have just taken my time. I would have also known that we were not compatible nor were our life missions. Reflecting back, I should have run but I didn't. If I have to pay the price for stupidity, I guarantee she won't dictate that for which I pay. This being the reason I blame myself, not her. I blame myself for allowing her to use me. I also blame myself for thinking at some point she would change her flirty ways. The lesson was taught and learned!

Kylie began sleeping with my boy Chip and God only knows what else she was up to. At first, I had no idea that this was going on. I trusted all my bruhs, although I did not know Chip and Al as well as I knew Derrick and Les. Thus far, I had no reason not to trust any of them.

This one particular day, I arrived home early from work and found Kylie talking on her phone using the speakerphone in my room. It was obvious she was speaking with a guy. She was all giggles while she put lotion on her body. I assumed she was preparing to leave for work. What got my attention was the familiarity of the voice. I leaned up against the door and listened. I knew the voice and the person attached to it. I instantly got pissed, but I knew I had to stay calm. I entered my bedroom door after I listened to a part of the conversation between the two.

I cleared my throat before I entered saying, "Hey Chip what's up bruh? She'll be there in a minute to bless your dick, player. No need in her lying any further or making up anything to tell me. You can have her dog." He hung up his end as she sat looking at me with tears in her eye's pleading her case. "GET OUT!" I shouted.

Kylie had the nerve to not want to leave. I had to threaten to call the police in order to get her to move close to the door. I pushed her out and slammed my door closed. I made sure to lock the door before returning to my room and collecting personal items she had at my residence. I wanted to throw them right out the door with her. I collected everything I could find, exited my room, returning to find her sitting on my couch. I almost shit my pants. This chic is super crazy.

"Didn't I just put you out of my house Kylie?"

"Yes, you did, but I had a key made so that I could gain access when or if I ever needed," she confessed with no shame. "Baby, what do you want for dinner?" she asked.

"DINNER!" I yelled. "Bitch, hit the damn door NOW! Give me my damn keys and leave! If you do not get out of my damn house, you will regret it!"

I can't believe how unbothered she acted. She sat back further on my couch as I paced back and forth launching threats.

"Come sit next to me Tru, and let's discuss this like adults," Kylie said with a calmness that would have scared Satan himself.

I looked at her without saying a word. I could not believe her boldness; I have never seen this side of her. I reached for my phone in order to call the police. I dialed 9-1-... before I saw something in my peripheral flying my way. I hit that last number one and laid the phone down on my counter. I looked on the floor to see what had just narrowly missed me and saw that it was a small knife.

"9-1-1 what's your emergency? Hello..."

I could hear the police on the line, but she couldn't. I wanted the incident recorded by them without her knowledge.

"Get out Kylie Ellis!" I needed them to know her first and last name. This is unbelievable. I refuse to believe you are trying to kill me in my own house. I am pressing charges on your crazy ass. I can't wait until the police get here.

"Well," she began. "You will have to prove what you claim I did first, and secondly, you need to call the police in time enough for them to catch me."

She had the audacity to think and then say those exact words. Not only did she say it, but she said it with confidence and cockiness. She had no idea that the call was already made.

Knock...Knock ... "Police!"

I rushed to open the door allowing the police access. I tried explaining what was going on, and that I wanted her removed. Kylie sat calm and cool like a crazy person would. The police approached her asking for her identification. When she opened her wallet, my bank card fell out and hit the floor. I asked her how she got my bank card out of my wallet?

"Honey, you let me use it, remember," Kylie said.

"I never allowed anyone access to my money nor any of my cards," I said to Officer Jackson.

While they took her statement, I called to check my balance.

"What the hell, Kylie! You stole five thousand dollars out of my account! So, let me get this straight, while the police are here as witnesses. Not only have you cheated on me with my boy, but you stole money from my account too?" Who has the papers I need to sign in order for me to press charges? Her ass needs to be hauled away! Is anyone listening around here! I am the victim dammit! I was assaulted, robbed of money and merchandise, and no one has asked me a damn thing! Escort that bitch to jail!"

"Calm down Mr. Livingston, we will be with you in a minute," responded raggedy ass Officer Roberts.

It was something about Officer Roberts that wasn't sitting right with me. I stood by my sink waiting for them to wrap up and escort her off my premises. After forty-five minutes of me being patient, they took Kylie away in handcuffs. I was instructed to take her to civil court about my money by the other officer, his name was Officer Jackson. I was also instructed to create a list of missing items to give to my attorney. Hopefully, I can recoup them or the money as well in court. Raggedy ass Officer Roberts told me to file for a restraining order, quote unquote, if I'm scared.

As officer Roberts escorted Crazy Kylie out, she had the nerve to mumble loud enough for me to hear, "He made this poor woman crazy. He is a HOE just like his boys! His day will come."

"Excuse me Officer Roberts, first of all, I have never met you a day in my life. Nor do I recall your name mentioned by any friends of mine. I am a hard-working man who has no time for raggedy, leeching, thieving, or cheating ass females. Nor do I have time to argue with irrelevant one's either. With that being said, enjoy your day!"

Chapter One

A Year Later
Dr. Tru Livingston

"Hey Tru, what's up man?" Chip asked.

"What's going on Chip? I have not heard from you in a while, this is definitely an unexpected call. More like a shocker."

"Tru, I wanted to apologize man. I was wrong as hell for messing around with your girl. We both bear responsibility for that dumb mess. I should not have ever messed around with that nasty crazy freak. That crazy bitch harassed and stalked all my side hoes. Man, I couldn't get any sex from none of my side pieces for weeks after she stalked and harassed them. I almost put on a dress and a wig and fought the strong hoe myself. I applaud you for enduring her nonsense for a year," Chip rambled off.

"Look man, we are good. I was mad at first because you knew she was my girl and living at my spot. We were getting serious. Yet, what happened was supposed to happen. Both of y'all were supposed to be exposed. If it weren't with you, she would have been doing that mess with someone else. No telling what else or who else she was doing behind my back. You saved me time and money."

Chip and I laughed and reminisced for a few more minutes. We ended the call with him promising to meet me and our other bruhs out later. I needed to get a move on it but was stuck in thought. It has been an entire year since I walked away from Kylie. During this year, I was able to retrieve most of my five thousand dollars from her, but none of my items. I am satisfied with what I did get. It was more of a lesson than anything. I have money, so money is no big deal. It was the principle behind what she did.

I am an educated professional that has no time for jail nor what I consider "hood drama". I've never even had a speeding ticket, let alone a fight. I am an OB/GYN. A gynecologist for those of you who do not know what it is. I have practiced for fifteen years. I refuse to be used or misused. I try treating any woman I date or spend time with respectfully. Someone must have truly hurt Kylie in her life. This would be the only acceptable reason I could think of for her to try and play me. What she will soon realize is I am not for play. It's one thing for her to be messing around with my boy behind my back. But stealing from a person who gave you anything you wanted, and then some, and expecting them to allow you to cheat and steal sounds foolish.

Kylie had too many struggles going on at one time. She needed to pick one. I told her to let Chip handle all of her bull crap. I changed my number three times, blocked her from calling me private and stopped her from stalking my home. I have had a restraining order for an entire year. I had to remind her that she did this to herself. She assumed I would never find out or catch on to her trying to run a game on me. The killing part was, during that time she would stay at my house more than she stayed at her own. I found out through a cousin of hers I met one night after we broke up, that she had two adult daughters and an adult son that she never even spoke of nor have a relationship with. I used to ask her about her family, and she would lie saying that her parents lived out of the state. She swore she had no real family. According to her cousin, Kylie's parents lived in the suburbs of our same city. She also has two younger sisters as well. Her daughters were away at college and the cousin never mentioned her son or sister's whereabouts.

Let me get my ass up and into the office. I have appointments starting at eight o'clock this morning and the last one is at five p.m. It's Friday and I want to swing by "Club Vibe" tonight. They are having spoken word and a new R and B artist whose performance starts at eight. I better make a note on my calendar to call Derrick, Les, and Al to see if they want to roll or meet me there. I am sure if they think a bunch of fat asses will be there, they will beat me in there and get us front row seats.

Chapter Two

The Appointment

I arrived at the office right before my first appointment. I had enough time to scrub my hands and brief myself on my new patients file before heading in. I knocked gently announcing myself before opening the door. I was at a loss for words as I entered the room. I was light weight embarrassed from becoming tongue tied and forgetting my own name. She was so beautiful that my dick got hard as hell and began to throb. I tried covering myself with her file praying she hadn't noticed. I reintroduced myself once the awkwardness of what I did vanished.

"Hello, I am Dr. Tru Livingston, and you are?"

"Hello Dr. Livingston. My name is Tess Smith, nice to finally meet you."

"Finally?" I asked.

"Yes, finally. I arrived in town over three months ago. A friend of mine highly recommended you. I needed an OBGYN I could trust, and my girl said you were the best," she stated.

"Wow, well tell your girl I said thank you for the great reference."

I began by asking her what brought her in today? I went on with the formalities inquiring about her medical history as well as her family's medical history. Tess answered as best she could. She had no idea about her parent's medical information, only her grandparents. I watched her plump lips pronounce every syllable, and her perfect teeth gleamed as she smiled. I looked in her eyes at the pain, yet she had an undeniable glow. She had beautiful hazel eyes. Her locks were long and curly framing her face perfectly. Her skin was like a dark chocolate hue.

"Do I need to reschedule?" she asked, snapping me out of my trance.

"No, no, please excuse me Ms. Smith. I apologize I never do this. I am so ashamed. What were you asking me?"

She smiled as she jokingly said, "Awe now the Mrs. must have put it on you last night."

We both began laughing.

"I wish there was a Mrs., I am single and have not dated in a year," I said.

Her mouth dropped as she said, "No shit!"

"No shit," I repeated.

"Well, Dr. Livingston, I need a pap smear and I also need my breast checked. I had a small cyst in my left breast that I had evaluated four or five months ago, but I am still a little sore."

I stood and pulled out a gown as she continued speaking.

"Ms. Smith, change into this gown. Put it on with the opening in the front. I will also get you a blanket to cover up. I will return when I think you have finished. Any questions?"

"None," Tess replied.

Chapter Three

Tess

Damn he is fine as hell. My girl was right. Oh, I am definitely about to get naked for Dr. Livingston. I hope I don't get horny during my exam. It has been exceedingly difficult dating and trusting again. My life has gone in a direction that I wouldn't have dreamed of going. Sometimes we do what we have to do to get what we need to get. I guess you can call it "fake it until you make it". Well, I've made it and am still faking it. I own my heart and I will never allow any man at this point to destroy me to build himself up. Don't get me wrong, I will definitely play the game, just know that this Queen won't be trumped. Ever since I went through all of that hell with Darnell, I decided that I was going to be my own main focus. Improving who I am is a priority. Being in an abusive relationship, be it physical or mental, can be life changing. My heart is hardened. One day, I may let someone in, but until that day I will fake it to get what I want and need.

I came back home to establish my roots back in the city without distractions. Lord please don't let my whorish ways surface unless it's beneficial.

I've been trying to keep things in perspective. Especially since I am officially in grad school, which is one of the main reasons I moved back. I need to stay focused on my goals and not on any specific man. My major is Criminal Justice who has proven to be exceedingly difficult. That does not include me performing some nights. I perform in order to have extra money to pay my bills. I also take on other odd gigs that pay me well. My bills need to be paid by any means necessary.

Back to Mr. Tru Livingston. I need to cut all of this flirting out, seriously. This is exactly how I ended up in my last couple of relationships. One was fake and the other was abusive. Darnell was a mental and physical abuser. He was the one who changed my outlook on men and life. I met Darnell in high school. I was with him on and off while in college. When he found out that I was accepted into grad school, his entire attitude and personality changed. Against my better judgment, we moved in together. He became possessive and abusive, both verbally and physically. He cheated constantly and threatened to end my life if I attempted to leave him. Darnell would bring women to our home and have sex with them under my nose. One time he tried to make me participate in some freaky threesome with him and I refused. He beat me and stomped me leaving me laying in the middle of the floor bleeding out of every whole. I thought I was dead, and he must have too. I awoke what seemed like hours later and was able to call my brother to take me to the hospital. I really did not want to involve my brother or anyone for that matter. I allowed Darnell's behavior, and I became accustomed to it out of fear. My brother was a street nucca. He had just got back on the streets from doing nine years on Rikers. He was looking at a double life sentence. He hired the best attorney's money could buy, and they got him off. No bodies and no weapons equal no murder. He was found guilty of robbery and transporting dope because he was snitched on. He was sentenced to fifteen years and served nine.

This being the reason I did not want him involved. There were a few other reasons as well. The biggest one was the fact that I knew personally that he killed several people and has never caught a case for any of them. My brother's name is Tyler Asencio, same mother, different fathers. The streets call him Casper because any witness, evidence, or case against him vanished. There was one exception who happened to be the one who did the snitching. My brother was set up and served time for the trap.

After Darnell beat and abused me, I was hospitalized for three weeks and then transported into a rehabilitation facility for several months. I had to learn to walk again. Darnell broke one of my kneecaps, a few bones in my back, fractured my ribs, broke my nose, and knocked out a few of my teeth. My brother Casper swore that Darnell would pay for it all. He would pay with his life or monetarily, but he would definitely pay. Casper came to visit me daily. He assisted me during therapy and rehabilitation. After I was released from the rehabilitation center, my brother moved me into his home, and we resided together almost two full weeks before he had me moved. He hooked me up in a setup that I could only come up from. I had a furnished rehabilitation room with the best equipment, it was beautifully furnished. I had a 24-hour cleaning service and health aide. I received a new Cadillac truck and my teeth repaired.

One day we were heading to the store to pick up a few items. This gave me the perfect opportunity to thank him and ask him where he was getting all this money he was spoiling me with. I thanked him for everything he'd done for me and expressed how much I appreciated his love and support.

"You're welcome," he responded. Not another word was said by him.

"Brother, may I ask you a question?"

"Sure," he responded.

"Where are you getting all of this money to do all these wonderful things?"

My brother said nothing. We sat in silence for five minutes. Those five minutes felt like five hours.

"I do not make promises I do not keep," is all he said.

My next question was, "Is he alive?"

"Yes," my brother responded.

I left the topic alone as we arrived in the mall's parking lot.

Chapter Four

Dr. Tru Livingston
The Exam

Knock...Knock

"May I enter?"

"Yes, you may, Dr. Livingston," Tess said.

I opened the door with the intention of acting more professionally this time around. I had a pep talk with myself in my office before entering. I even went into my personal bathroom and jacked off in hopes of not getting another boner while I did my job.

"Welcome back," she said with a smile.

"Thank you," I responded as I pulled a stool up and sat in order to begin the exam.

"Ms. Smith, I am going to need you to slide to the end of the table. That's it. Now put each leg in a stirrup. The process will be a bit uncomfortable, but hopefully this will not take long."

I retrieved a tube of K-Y and put a small amount on my gloved fingers and parted her legs. As I went to insert my fingers into her vagina beginning the exam, I noticed how tight she was. I heard her breaths; the sound was sweet and innocent.

"Are you okay?" I asked.

"Better than okay," she responded.

I entered her sweetness with my fingers again, feeling for any abnormalities. I felt her gyrating on my fingers in small circles. I ignored her moans. She had the prettiest pussy I had ever seen. I let her gyrate a minute longer as I acted as though I was clueless. I should have stopped her right then and there, but I didn't.

My dick was so hard it was beginning to hurt. She opened her eyes and looked at me begging me to continue. In all of my years of practicing this was my first. I verbally denounced the idea knowing that I could get stripped of my license and lose my job. She removed her legs from the stirrups as she sat up in front of me holding on to my fingers. Her grip was tight, she made it clear she did not want my fingers removed. She grinded on them while staring me in my eyes. She apologized seductively, yet she kept going. She reached down with her other hand and grabbed my thick dick. She rubbed and stroked him as I said no and tried pulling away. Tess stood up facing me in her bareness grabbing my waste as she ground her pussy on my dick.

"DAMN!" I thought and said aloud. She began unzipping my pants. I again said, "No, please stop," although in my mind, I was like damn baby get this dick.

She was able to pull out my dick as she got on her knees and sucked every bit of cum I had up there from last year. By then, I needed to be up in her wet pussy. I laid her back against my better judgement, and I fucked her. She felt amazing and I felt myself about to explode, until I heard a knock at the door.

"I am finishing the exam," was all I said loud enough for whomever that was knocking to hear.

My nurse replied, "Room five has been waiting forty-five minutes passed their appointment, sir."

"Ask them if they are able to give me ten more minutes. I am wrapping up now."

"Okay," she answered back, sounding frustrated.

Tess and I finished up, both feeling awkward and embarrassed. I asked her if I could have her number as a courtesy. This has never happened to me before, hell I had no idea what I was supposed to do at that moment. We exchanged numbers and she left. Here I go again, I thought. The lesson I was being taught by messing with Kylie based on her beauty was not learned. I finally just said forget it, women rule the world. I moved on with my day preparing to hook up with my boys later tonight.

Chapter Two

Club Vibe

I walked into Club Vibe and was extremely impressed by the renovations. I maneuvered my way through the crowd looking for my boys and hoping I could get a drink on my way to a seat. Derrick stood up and waved his arms until he caught my eye. I made my way toward the front stage where they all sat laughing and drinking.

"What's up Tru?" asked Les and Al.

"What's up fellas?" I responded.

Chip and Derrick gave me daps as I took a seat facing the stage. We had less than five minutes before the show began. Thank God they had bottles of Dom already purchased on the table and had a class on chill for me. We all poured and made a toast just as the lights dimmed.

"Ladies and Gentlemen, I'd like to welcome you to Club Vibe. Tonight's M.C. will be the 330's own comedian, Curly James. Please help me welcome the infamous Curly James to the stage!"

Applause...Applause

"Thank you everyone. Tonight is guaranteed to be a night to remember. We have special guests performing spoken word as well as the hottest R&B band in the city performing tonight. First up will be a spoken word from Akron's own, 3Relli. Please help me welcome Three Relli to the mic with her hot piece entitled "My Thoughts'.

Applause...Applause

"Hello everyone. I want to take you deep into my mind where my thoughts are too deep to remember, yet I remember being in thought. Dreaming about what reality really means, or if reality was what is real to me. I have faith that the unknown is a spiritual realm in which the human mind will never comprehend. I believe that as human beings we are spiritually guided from within, not from without."

"Before we became a seed, we were a thought, brought into existence by a creator of all things. In the beginning was a word. The world is a mystery, a puzzle with pieces that will never fit in human thought. Books were written, stories told. The life of the creator plagiarized by many. The answer is in the realm where the truth lie. Our minds could never think on the level of the almighty. Therefore, we pass down what is not written, fourth guessing the prophecies from prophets who were gifted with the word. It is easier to believe some human mind's explanation versus a true word that's meant to be stood on and not thought out. My thoughts are too deep for you to comprehend A WORD!"

"Wow, now that was deep. Thank you 3Relli, that was fire. Next up is Just Us, featuring Tess. She will be singing their new release FUCK LOVE! Please help me show "Just Us" some love y'all!"

"Damn, that was deep. I may stay back after this to see if she has a book or other poetry she may be selling. I would love to support her work."

"I bet you would," Derrick and Les laughingly said.

Al agreed with me. Although he looked like his mind was somewhere else.

"Shush!" We heard in the distance.

I immediately stopped talking in order to hear her beautiful voice. I turned my chair all the way around to see the person attached to the voice. The band was amazing. The lead singer had a voice like Erykah Badu. She didn't just sing; she sang that song...Tess was the epitome of a beautiful woman.

I can't deny the fact that we don't belong together.

The love between us bae, dissolved in stormy weather.

I tried to hold you down, you turned and pushed away.

I kneeled and prayed to gawd for a clear and brighter day.

I miss you baby, but back up and give me fifty feet.

You don't get it like that. Fuck Love.

We want what we want, in life it's just a fact.

Fuck Love, no love in order you straight just fuckin back.

You said you want to chill, not recognizing real...

You choked on all the facts, now you want your baby back.

The game doesn't work like that, I gave you all I had.

You had a point to prove, now you're screaming.

It's yo bag of tricks ... I'm not your treat.

I skip games on messy mess.

Next time you want to play,

Play checkers don't play chess.

I miss you baby, but back up and give me fifty feet, cause you ain't got it like that. FUCK LOVE!

Everyone in the building was on their feet applauding. The poets came out and performed a few more pieces as well as Tess and her band. They put on a show well worth admission. We had a while before the last call, so I excused myself from the table as soon as I saw Tess take a seat at the bar. I wanted to speak as well as compliment her, her group, and the poets on their performances.

"The show was amazing," I stated as I walked up behind Tess and whispered in her ear. She never turned nor jumped.

She replied by asking, "Which one?"

I laughed a little because again, I was caught off guard with her wit. "Both," I came back with.

She turned and looked me dead in my eyes, and said in a matter-of-fact tone, "If that was all it took to impress you, wait until you see what I have in store for you next."

I froze with a question mark look on my face. I wasn't sure whether I was supposed to take that in a threatening manner or in a flirty way. I just stood there looking dumb until she got up out of her seat, pulled me into her and whispered, "Meet me in thirty minutes."

Tess slipped a piece of paper in my hand and walked off into the crowd. I walked back over to the table as the bruhs were trying to talk to a few females at the table next to ours.

I took my seat and looked down into my hand at what was written on the paper. I didn't recognize the street, so as the guys continued being distracted by the ladies next to us, I googled the address. It came up as the Embassy Hotel on the east side of town. I smiled at the thought, yet on the other end, I needed to say something just in case this was a set up. I signaled for the server. When she came, I asked her to close my tab after I ordered another round seeing that we drank the Dom they ordered before I got here. I placed a wing order to go, and I was ready to bounce.

"Is there anything else?" the server asked before leaving.

"No, and thank you," I said.

I took that opportunity to let the bruhs know that I had a date and that I was about to bounce. All inquiring minds wanted to know who the mystery woman was, but that part I wasn't telling. I just told them to listen out for a text or call from me within the hour. If they didn't hear from me, come to the Embassy on the east side prepared for war. We said our goodbyes just in time. The server came with the drinks and my food.

Chapter Six

The Hook Up

I entered my car and immediately entered the address into Google's directions just in case I got lost. The anticipation of seeing Tess again had my stomach in knots. I prayed that I didn't get the bubble guts. Every time I get nervous that is exactly what happens. I decided to turn the radio on and listen to some "for lovers only". They were jamming. I began singing in the car imagining that I was singing to Tess. I must have drifted into lala land because all I heard was beeping. My car swerved too far in the speed lane and almost caused a collision. That was too close I thought. My exit was approaching so I checked my breath and armpits to make sure that I was good, and I was. I saw the sign as I exited the freeway for the Embassy. At the light I needed to make a right and it was right there.

As I entered the parking lot, I began to wonder what the hell I was doing. I have no clue as to who she is, nor anything else about her but how she looks naked. I pray that this is not a set up and that she is seriously a nice person.

I walked in and entered the elevator nervous as hell. I exited on the second floor and looked for room 201. It was the first room on the left. I knocked gently expecting her to be different from the person I was intimate with earlier. To be honest, I really couldn't tell you anything outside of how stupid I felt and how stupid I must have looked. When she opened the door, she was all smiles.

"Hello Tru," she stated.

"Hello Ms. Tess," I replied.

She grabbed me by the hand gently and pulled me in. Her room was spacious and had a living room area with a television and a small CD player. It also had a kitchenette with an apartment sized refrigerator and stove, as well as a small sink with a few cabinets. It was cute. The bedroom had a queen-size bed with a bathroom and television. We decided to sit in the living room area because I wanted to talk. I needed to take my time and really get to know her. She poured us some wine as we made a toast to our newfound friendship.

I began the conversation with an apology for my unprofessional behavior. I tried to explain to her that I had never met anyone like her before. I told her briefly about my ex-Kylie, but never gave her Kylie's name. We spoke about my family, my profession, and me having no kids, etc.

Tess didn't hide a thing. She went into detail about the family she was raised by, not being reared by her mother, her relationship with her siblings, and her job and school. Tess claims that she goes out with another guy every now and then, but they haven't had sex yet. She elaborated on her abusive past relationship and what affects it has had on her personal life. She also apologized for what happened today explaining that this is why she invited me here tonight. I asked her why not her place, why a hotel?

"Tru, this is a safe place. We don't actually know each other enough to be having sex, let alone know where one another lives. None of this makes sense, nor how I feel about you in only one day. It feels like we were destined to be with one another. Like on that show, Love At First Sight. This is scary for me."

"I understand because the feelings are definitely mutual," I responded.

She continued with her confessions about tonight. She began telling me that during her performance she spotted me. At first, she claimed that she wanted to run. Then she confessed that she talked herself into putting her big girl panties on and continuing with the show. We both laughed, and then my tipsy self-asked her to show me what big girl panties look like. She looked at me like she could devour me in one bite and said, "Follow me."

I jumped up before she could finish her statement, like I was the thirstiest guy on the planet. I almost slobbered at the thought of seeing her naked again off the clock. No interruptions, no nothing. Tess leaned over and inserted a cd from this singer, Ro James. The name of the song she chose was, Permission. She stood up and took off her shirt and pants and then pressed play. As we both listened to the words, she danced her way between my legs as I leaned back a little admiring her beauty.

"With your permission, I just want to spend a little time with you...With your permission...tonight I want to be a little me on you."

Father, please don't let this be my imagination. If it is, please let me be a beast, I prayed. Thank you, Amen. I stood up and started dancing with her to this cut. I held her close but softly, not wanting to be too aggressive. I wanted her to find comfort in my arms and feel secure. It must be working because she laid her head on my chest and held me like her life depended on it.

Everything was going great. I leaned in to kiss her sweet soft lips. She grabbed me by my head and held me like she never wanted to let me go. I turned her around and laid her on the bed gently, not wanting her to stop kissing me. My dick was stiff and throbbing. I stopped kissing her lips and explored her neck, kissing her all over her face softly. I went a little lower kissing down to her voluptuous breast. Her nipples were large and perfectly shaped. I sucked and nibbled on them as I began rubbing on her clit. My goal was to get it wet and hot for me to devour next. She wiggled and moaned making sure I knew she approved of what I was doing.

I eased down her stomach, sucking her navel working my way to her sweetness. I stood up, pulled her to the edge of the bed, pushed her knees apart and dove right in. I sucked, licked, and massaged her pussy with my tongue. She squirted as I rubbed and sucked her juices out. I wasn't finished. I took my time going back in as I stiffened my tongue and tongue fucked her until she couldn't take it anymore. She pulled my face in, almost suffocating me as she pumped my face and began to cum once more. It drove both of us crazy as I began slurping and sucking her dry. I rubbed her clit around with my tongue putting my finger in her ass as she moaned loud enough to wake up sleeping beauty. She squirted so much she almost took out my eye. She rolled from under me lightly pushing me off. She got down and had me stand in front of her. She took me slowly. Tess licked and sucked from the tip to the base. I am not sure at this moment how she was able to get it all in her mouth, but she did it and it felt damn good! She sped up some, moistening my shaft. I couldn't take it anymore, I had to feel her insides. We switched positions so that I was able to mount her from the back. Just as I slid in her wetness, we heard a big boom! It frightened us both because we had no idea of what or who it could be.

Chapter Seven

The Intruders

I was able to see three masked individuals as they ran in toting guns. I was unable to move fast enough to either hide or grab a weapon. There was nothing I could pick up or use to defend Tess or myself before we were attacked. I just remember individuals dressed in all black. They ran in and began beating, stomping, and kicking us. I tried fighting back at first but was overpowered. I caught a glimpse of Tess bawled up like a baby being pistol whipped. She made little to no noise. I screamed out like a chic, that crap hurt. Those hits were hurting like crazy. Tess was taking those hits like a champ, and I acted like a chump. The harder she was hit, the tighter she bawled up. After what seemed like several minutes of being beaten, we were tied up and gagged. Out of all times, Tess gave them a tough time when they tried tying her up. I didn't, I did not have the energy. I could hear one of the intruders telling her to stop tensing up and to sit still. I just knew my bones were broken and I was half dead. Blood was everywhere; it was a real crime scene. I was in so much pain, it hurt to even think. Yet, I thought back to feeling eerie and not being sure if this was a set up or not. I prayed that my boys questioned my whereabouts and came to look for me seeing that I never called. I looked back over at Tess who happened to have shed a couple tears and continued to resist. I wanted her to know that we would be okay, but speaking was not an option. Our eye's had to do all the talking. The intruders looked through drawers in the room and headed into the sitting area. I silently wondered why they came and what they were looking for. There is no clarity for any of this. We heard the door close and dead silence.

I just laid still, thinking about how this all went down and wondering why. I continued to lay in one place playing dead just in case they returned. I was able to peek a little out of my now swollen eyes and watched on as Tess finagled her beat up body loose. Her body was tense when she was being tied, at least that's what I heard one say. She was able to relax her body which made her body shrink. She rotated her wrist back and forth to loosen them. I watched as she sat her body up enough to rub her wrist across some jagged wood on the edge of the dresser. She repeated pulling her wrist apart and rubbing until she was able to free herself. Tess then removed the duct tape off of her mouth and called 9-1-1. After hanging up with the police, she made another call. Whomever she called; she began speaking in an unfamiliar language. I stayed still as she began screaming and hollering. I did identify a few of the words but didn't understand the context. All I could think of was damn, here we go again, pussy got me caught up.

If I live through this, I am thinking about becoming celibate, all of this relationship stuff is too much work. I watched as she limped pacing back and forth before realizing she had never tried assisting me.

"Damn!" she said out loud.

Tess jumped like a lightbulb had just gone off inside of her head. She began slicing the rope with a little nail filer knife after she removed the tape from my mouth. Tess ran and got me a cold glass of water and a cold rag.

She rubbed my face and asked, "Are you okay? Do you want to call anyone?"

"I'm good. Can you hand me my phone off the nightstand?" I said.

After placing a call to my boys, I thought to ask her how she was feeling through swollen lips.

She apologized and said, "I am sore, but I will live. You on the other hand look like you need medical attention."

"I'm good," I responded. "Nothing, a little ice and rest can't cure."

She disagreed and told me I may need an x-ray for my ribs. We both just sat there looking off into the distance until Tess gave me a look of true confusion.

"I hope my ex-boyfriend is not behind any of this. Do you remember I told you I had a crazy ex-boyfriend?" Tess asked. Before I could answer she continued, "The more I think about it, this has his jealous, ass name written all over it. He has tried as well as threatened to kill me several times while my brother was away," she stated.

Tess went on rehashing her traumatic experience with her ex-boyfriend. She continued with how controlling he was with uncontrollable anger issues. She explained how he used excuses to beat her constantly or abuse her in some fashion. Tess became numb to the beatings and his abusive ways over time. She knew not to cry out or allow him to see her cry. She stated that she always kept a small weapon on her just in case. Normally it was a fingernail file, which was small enough to fit in her bra unnoticeable.

"I am not sure if he has found me or if someone is after you," she stated. Tess looked over at me and said, "Tru unless we are being followed, how would anyone know where we are? I didn't tell anyone where we would be. That is why this is truly bothering me. I have one other call to make and that is to my brother," she mumbled.

"To your brother?" I thought, trying to put this puzzle together.

"Yes," Tess began explaining. "The last time my ex beat me and left me for dead, my brother had just come home from prison. My brother came to our house and picked me up. He didn't call the police or for an ambulance because he wanted to personally transport me to the hospital. We spoke briefly about this."

"Yes, I remember," I answered.

"My brother stayed with me at the hospital, assisted with my therapy and paid for everything. He made sure I was able to get my strength back and get back on my feet. He also handled my ex. I just want to make sure that he was handled permanently or find out if he has resurfaced."

As Tess spoke with her brother, I thought about my own drama. Could Kylie have anything to do with this even though I haven't seen or heard from her, or did one of my bruhs set me up? I did tell them I had a date tonight and if they hadn't heard from me within the hour to come to the Embassy ready for war. My thoughts were interrupted by

Tess's conversation with her brother screaming through the phone and a knock on the door.

The bruhs arrived at the same time the police did. Naturally, they were asked to show their I.D. and asked why they were there. After that little episode, they made their way over to me with genuine concern. Al went to go retrieve ice, Les grabbed towels and looked for ointment and Tylenol. I was barely able to laugh when he asked if we had any K-Y jelly he could use. Derrick checked on Tess and sat next to me listening to her statement to the police. My boy Chip, I noticed, just stood back watching everything and everybody. Tess gave the police an ear full but didn't tell them everything. The police wrapped up just as the paramedic and the manager of the hotel entered. The paramedic looked us both over as the manager spoke with the police. They suggested that I get transported to the hospital for a few x-rays. I agreed that I would go to the hospital, but that one of my friends would bring me.

After speaking with the police, the manager spoke with us both, extending his apologies for the incident. He also made it clear that his hotel does not tolerate this type of misconduct. He'd personally check us out of his hotel and refund us our stay. We both thanked him and asked for time to gather our items.

He agreed and left like the others. Once the manager left, the bruhs, Tess, and I remained still. We were discussing what happened when we heard another knock at the door. Tess opened the door and there stood her brother with about ten other gangster type dudes.

"Oh shit!" I heard the bruhs say. Which was exactly what I was thinking.

Chapter Eight

That's The Way Love Goes

Time has flown by, and it has been almost six weeks since the incident. I am healing up fairly well. I ended up having Tess's brother take me to the hospital because he insisted on her getting checked out also. I had a few bruised ribs, a loosened tooth and more swelling than anything. The doctors advised me to get plenty of rest. So, I took off work for a few weeks and slept, iced, and relaxed. After a couple of days, I got up and moved around. I had to handle some business. I had a security system installed and changed my locks while I had time. I also went to the bank and moved some of my money around. I opened up another account at a new bank transferring a substantial portion for extra safety measures. I bought a safe to put in my hidden little vault in my home. I also used this time to go to the police department to see if they had any leads. The dentist isn't my favorite place, but I went to have my teeth checked. It felt like a couple were knocked loose, but they were checked so I am all good. My family doctor was next up. My doctor wanted to re-examine my ribs, so she also ordered up-to-date x-rays. She wanted to make sure my healing process was on track.

The police have not gotten any closer to solving that mystery beating than we received. They retrieved footage from the hotel cameras showing the intruders entering the hotel and exiting on our floor. It showed the three entering our room, as well as two other intruders standing outside our door. The detective zoomed in and noticed a mystery person in all black wearing a mask. The mystery person stood at the far end of the hall. When the intruders ran out, the mystery person walked off in the opposite direction. The issue at hand was the quality of the video recording. With what they had at present; it was hard to zoom in on faces. I was assured by the detective that we would soon have answers. A digital videographer will be arriving in a couple of days. Looking at that footage and reliving that day attributed to the nightmares I had begun having after I put Kylie out.

The day at the hotel was the worst day of my life. I just knew I was going to get killed two times in one day or beat half to death twice. When Tess's brother and his rough looking friends entered the room, they came ready to end my life and the bruhs lives, especially after they saw Tess's face and damage. It took Tess getting upset and actually crying before she was able to calm her brother and his crew down. She was able to explain what happened. Tess went into detail with them about the things she noticed. She didn't tell the police everything she noticed about the intruders. One intruder had a teardrop tattoo under their right eye, and another had on contacts. She took notice because their eyes were two totally unusual colors. A contact may have fallen out in the room somewhere.

Tess found out that her ex was still breathing for the moment. Before Tess's brother left to take us to the hospital, he told his gangster friends to make sure Tess's ex-Darnell was their first target. They swore they wouldn't rest until they hunted him down. The gangsters were on the prowl and looking for any information they could on who did this. They discussed needing a plan of action and suddenly stopped talking and began observing the bruhs. I noticed how her brother kept looking at Chip and Al like he knew them and didn't like them one bit. Chip stood back acting like he didn't feel their heat and Al faked like he was in the conversation with Tess and the other bruhs. The rest of us felt their heat, so I know they did. No one said a word, but everyone observed. I took mental notes.

After leaving the police department, I decided to go home, drink a glass of wine, and relax. I thought about checking on Tess since I have not spoken to her in a couple of days. Tess answered the phone on the second ring as though she was happy to hear from me.

"Hello sexy," I began.

"Hello Tru, how are you feeling?" Tess replied.

"I am healing. I got out of the house today and handled some things. Other than that, I have just been relaxing."

"Same here," Tess answered back.

Tess went on to talk about her brother. She stated that her brother and a couple of his boys have been camped out over at her spot around the clock. She was unable to do anything but heal and chill. Tess and I laughed and talked for over two hours. I began to get tired, and I was buzzing off the wine. I woke straight up when Tess said, "I knew it was something I was supposed to ask you. My brother wants to know how you are associated with your friend that was standing off from everybody and the weird one sitting by me?"

"Huh? What does he mean?" I questioned.

"Well, my brother knows your friends and said they are shady," Tess replied.

"Let me just say this, and you can tell your brother or whatever. The one who was standing was my bruh who cheated with my crazy ex. It was around a year to the day that we met. I busted those two about a year later around the same time. I hadn't spoken to or seen him since. He reached out to apologize which was strange."

"Nothing is adding up," Tess added.

"It just appears to me that I may have to keep my eyes on a few people," I responded. "You can also tell your brother I am not with that mess they are on. I don't know what those dudes are into or what they do on a regular basis. We never hung like that," I told Tess.

Tess and I spoke for a few more minutes before I reiterated that I was tired and needed to lay down. We said our goodnights, and both hung up our lines. I plumped my pillows up and laid back, relaxing my mind, body, and soul.

I can't breathe or open my eyes! Oh my god, It feels like someone has my face covered with a pillow and applying pressure! Get off of me! I feel bound to something but can't figure out what that something is. I am unable to move any of my limbs. I am screaming for help but can't hear my cries! My life is spiraling out of control and there isn't anything

I can do to help myself! GOD, if you are listening, please help me! I cried silently and just laid still until I drifted.

The Bruhs

I awoke to the phone ringing. It was Al checking up on me. He, Derrick, and Les wanted to know if I wanted to hang out, seeing that I was only off work for a few more days. I was a little discombobulated when I first answered.

Al laughed and asked, "Is this bad timing?"

"Not really, I had another nightmare. I am making an appointment first thing in the morning to see Dr. Rose. Enough is enough."

"I am sorry to hear that you are still going through that shit bruh. You definitely need to get out of the house," Al said matter-of-factly.

"You might be right. Where are y'all trying to go?" I asked as though there were a lot of options for people our age.

"Bruh, we don't have many adult choices in this little ass city. The Vibe is where we will be. If you decide you want to go, we plan to meet up at 9:00 p.m.," Al said.

"Bet," was all I said.

We hung up our lines and I decided to get up, clean and get my day started. It felt like it was still yesterday, like I had just laid down.

Welp, first thing is first, let me call Dr. Rose's office and make an appointment. I then tightened up around here so that I can fix something to eat and bounce.

"Hello, this is Tru Livingston, I would like to make an appointment with Dr. Rose please."

"Hello Mr. Livingston, let me check her schedule for you. Would you like a morning or afternoon sir?"

"It doesn't matter," I responded. "Whatever you have open first is good for me," I continued.

"Her schedule is full for next month Mr. Livingston, but we can call you if someone cancels or needs to reschedule. If you need to be seen sooner, you can call us by 9:00 a.m. daily."

"I need to be seen as soon as possible. I will, thank you so much!"

Just as soon as I hung up my line, I heard a knock at the door. I walked over to look on my security screen and saw that it was a female. Her back was to the camera as though she was looking around out in front. I started smiling thinking damn, Tess! I opened the door; I almost had a heart attack. I tried slamming the door back before she placed her big ass foot in the door to prevent it from shutting.

"What the hell do you want Kylie? You are in violation of the restraining order. I am calling the police!" I yelled.

"No, please don't. I did not come to harm you or to cause any issues. I need to talk to you about something," she stated.

"I do not trust you, move!" I yelled.

I pushed her back hard enough for her to lose her footing and I shut the door. I called the police and reported her being in violation. As I spoke on the phone I watched as she brushed herself off, looked around mysteriously, and walked off briskly. She continued to look around until she reached a red Altima parked down a couple houses. She jumped in the driver's seat and pulled off. Just as she pulled off, the police pulled up. I opened the door and screamed that she was getting away. The police ignored me, telling me to calm down. They asked me questions I had no answers to. Such as, where does she live? The plate number on the Altima? What did she want to speak to me about? Was she threatening? Etcetera. Once they took the police report and left, I wasn't in the mood to do anything but drink. I called Al back and asked him to come and swoop me up for the club later.

"I will be ready," I stated. "I am just not up to driving."

"Cool," Al said. He stated that he would be at my house at 8:30 sharp.

As usual, we got to Club Vibe early enough to choose our seating. This time I suggested that we sit in the cut, away from everything so that we could see. We ordered a couple of bottles of Dom and Derek passed around his vape pen. We were all high as hell. We laughed and flirted with every girl that walked past us. The club was getting crowded, people were hitting the dance floor. When the clubs D.J. started playing DMX, "What They Really Want", we all jumped up and hit the dance floor grabbing whoever was available to dance. We were kicking it until we heard some commotion and looked in the direction of the crowd. It was Chip and Tess's brother going at it. I stopped in my tracks. Tess's brother was telling Chip that if he knew what was good for him that he would disappear. Chip was not the same Chip we knew. He was talking shit like a boss. He was telling Tess's brother that he wasn't going anywhere! If he wanted him gone then he knew the terms! Now my interest is peaked, what is really going on around here? I walked off the dance floor stepping closer to the confrontation so that I could clearly hear the exchange. Al, Derrick, and Les were right behind me peeping out the entire scene. The next thing we knew they locked up and started going in on one another. People were running and screaming. Next came the gunshots. We ran straight for the door and out the door once the fighting started. We heard gunshots from outside. People began running out the door. We saw some of the security pull Tess's brother and his crew out the side from where we were parked. They were hyped and still ready to fight. A few minutes later, Chip and a few dudes we had never seen before came out the front door. They loaded up in a white Telluride with silver tint and just sat facing the Vibe. Me and Al got in his car and leaned our seats back. Les and Derrick were parked next to us and did the same thing.

After waiting a few minutes to make sure that we would not be in a line of fire, we pulled off and went in the opposite direction. We decided to go somewhere and sit down and get something to eat. The Cracker Barrel was open, so we pulled in there, jumped out and stood in line waiting to be seated. None of us said more than two words until we sat down to order.

"Man, those nuccas on some bullshit," Derrick finally said.

"Right," Les agreed. "We are too grown for all this fake tough shit! What happened to going out and having an enjoyable time with the ladies and then going home. Everybody got guns and everyone is so damn hard! This shit is irritating as hell!"

"My exact thoughts," I said. "What got me messed up all the way up is Chip. When did that dude get tough?"

Derrick looked around at all of us and said, "Look, I care less about how tough that weird nucca got over night. I dropped my damn weed running. I am mad as hell!"

We all laughed, but I noticed Al wasn't saying much. There is too much weird stuff going on lately. After tonight, I am going to disappear for a minute. I will be going to work and back home, that's it. The vibes I am getting from Al and Chip are not good. After tonight, my list has Al and Chip as questionable as Kylie's stalking ass. Shit, they are already on the list. I need to stop smoking. I need a mental break from all this mess before I mess around and get killed or lose my job. We ate and knew it was time to go home.

Al didn't say too much of anything on our ride to my house.

"What's on your mind?"

"I'm good, this was all too overwhelming for me," Al responded.

"I understand," was all I said before we arrived at my house. "Thanks, bruh," I said before exiting his car.

I opened my door and entered my home. I was happy to be back home. I took a quick shower and laid across my bed trying to put the pieces to all this together. I concluded that I would hire a private investigator. I needed answers that I couldn't get. I can't trust anyone, so this would be my best bet. I felt a sense of relief as I drifted off into a deep sleep.

"Who are you? Show me your face and please tell me why do you continue to harass me? How are you getting in my home? Answer me DAMMIT! Get away from me, where is your face? STOP! I am calling the police! STOP, I can't breathe! Somebody please help me, please GOD help me!!"

Chapter Ten

The Help

I awoke out of another nightmare dripping in sweat and on the verge of a serious heart attack. My normal boring life has turned into a movie that I am unable mentally to be the star of. I jumped back in the shower and ended up staying up half the night. I needed to put a game plan together. Enough is enough and I am determined to stand up in this shit and not keep running from it. Nobody, and I mean nobody will dictate how I move! I have another day off before I have to head back to work, so I am going to do everything I need to do. It is too early to call Dr. Rose's office for an appointment. So, I am about to log in to Google and find a Private Investigator or an undercover detective, somebody is going to help me solve this bullshit. While I am on Google, I need to search out some truths about a few people. I will start with Tess and her brother. I've known Derrick and Les a lot longer than I have known Chip and Al. I am going to look up information on those two as well as Kylie.

I must have dozed off because I woke up after hearing my phone ring.

"Hello," I answered, sounding groggy."

"Hello and good morning Mr. Livingston, this is nurse Ms. Mitty. I was looking over your schedule for your return to work tomorrow, and saw you have a 7:30 a.m. Would you like to reschedule this patient for a later time or a different day?"

"No, Ms. Mitty, I will be in the office by 7:00 a.m. Thank you for checking."

"No problem Mr. Livingston," she responded. "Enjoy your day."

I immediately got back on my search. I researched Private Investigators, undercover police, and I googled everything. I wanted the best that money could buy. I found a firm that had high reviews and great references called Hodoh, Sanders and McLane. I immediately called and scheduled an appointment. Thank God they had a cancellation for today at 1:00p.m. I took it and planned to be there early. I also called the police department to see if there were any recent updates.

Detective Sharpey began, "Mr. Livingston, I think…"

The line went dead, and my power was out. I began switching the lights and going through to the kitchen checking the stove and refrigerator. I headed to my utility closet to check and see if the circuit was tripped. I switched each fuse back and forth, there was nothing. I went in my room and retrieved my pistol to go out and see what the hell was going on. I never got a license to shoot or carry, but I didn't care at the time. I headed outside and saw that the entire street was out. I breathed a sigh of relief knowing that it wasn't just me. The only other option I had was to leave as is. I decided to get myself something to eat and head on to my appointment. Hell, I need to be looking to move next. That damn house is going to be the death of me.

"Welcome Mr. Livingston to Hodoh, Sanders and McLane. How can we serve you?" asked the receptionist, Ms. Davis.

"Hello Ms. Davis, I have an appointment with Mr. Hodoh at 1:00p.m. I'm a little bit early."

"Oh, that's fine," she responded joyfully. "Please fill out this paperwork Mr. Livingston, and someone will be with you soon."

"Thank you," I responded.

After a few minutes had passed Ms. Davis offered me a beverage as well as a piece of fruit for a refreshment. I declined her offer because I picked up a bite to eat on my way here.

I watched as a prestigious young gentleman walked out and announced my name. I stood and raised my hand to say "here I am.' He shook my hand and walked me back into an office I soon found out was his. He unbuttoned his jacket and offered me a seat.

"Hello Mr. Livingston, my name is Brayland Hodoh. I am a Private Investigator and an ex-undercover detective. Let me tell you a little about myself. I left the police department after five years of doing undercover work for them, because I wanted to start up my own firm. I still periodically work hand in hand with them on different cases. I have high reviews because I get the job done. I am a man of many disguises. You wouldn't recognize me anywhere, unless I told you it was me. I find out any information I want to know, nothing is off limits for me. That is a little background on me. How may I help you today?"

I looked at him and chuckled a little. "Okay, so do you want the condensed version of events, or the longer?"

Mr. Hodoh laughed and said, "Give me what you got. Please do not leave out any details. They may not be pertinent to you, but they may be effective on my end."

I began telling him my story from the beginning. "Well, I used to date Kylie. We stopped dating over a year ago. I came home from work and walked in on her and Chip, a bruh, on the phone flirting. I told her to leave, and I put her ass out. I walked back out into my living room area, and noticed she was back in my home sitting on my couch. She had the nerve to let herself back in with a key she had made behind my back. While waiting for the police she also threw a small knife at me. She had no idea that I had the police on the line. I wanted to make sure the altercation was recorded, and I wasn't falsely accused. The police took statements. During their interview of Kylie, the police asked for identification. When she searched for her identification in her wallet, my bank card fell out. I called the bank and discovered she had taken five thousand dollars from me. After searching my home, I also found out she stole other things. I hired an attorney and retrieved most of my money back. I also got a restraining order on her, so I had not seen her for over a year. I started back having nightmares and feeling paranoid as though someone was entering my home. I changed the locks and bought security cameras. Things went from that to me meeting Tess Smith. I have been seeing Tess lately, not much though. I met her in my office. She claimed that she came to me because I came highly recommended. As stupid and as ignorant ass it sounds, I had sex with her in my office that very day. She came onto me while doing her exam. I couldn't help myself at the time, seeing that I was guilty of getting a hard on as soon as I walked in the exam room. I tried covering it up, but I don't think I did a decent job. We went over her medical history and her reason to be seen. I gave her a gown and left back out. I waited to return, giving her time to undress, and put on her gown. Once I returned and had her put her legs in the stirrups she began grinding on my fingers. I tried to ignore her advances until she sat herself up and pulled me in. We had sex, exchanged phone numbers, and went on our way."

"I ran into Tess later that same day at Club Vibe. My bruhs and I met up at the vibe to listen to some spoken word and a band called "Just Us." I was shocked to see Tess there and had no idea she sang in the band. After the show, I walked up to her and congratulated her on their performance. She thanked me, and afterward handed me a sheet of paper with an address on it and asked me to meet her there. I told my bruhs I had a date, and if they didn't hear from me in an hour, to come to that address ready for war. My bruh, Al, was acting a little different, but I chalked it up. I arrived at the address which turned out to be the Embassy Hotel. We had a wonderful time getting to know one another as we sat in the living room area of the room talking and laughing about our lives and chance encounters."

"After having a few drinks, we moved into the bedroom area and began doing what grown folks do. In the mist of having sex, we heard a BOOM! The door was knocked open by some masked intruders. There were three intruders that entered the room. They began beating Tess and me. After they beat us, they searched for something briefly and left. I could barely move. Tess was able to get loose. I watched her finagle herself out of the rope and remove the tape from her mouth. She then assisted me and made calls to the police. When the police arrived, so did the paramedics. I called and filled the bruhs in, and they arrived just as the police were finishing up. After the police questioned them as though they were suspects, they released them. The bruhs took seats and looked on at Tess as she filled them in on what happened. She began giving them details that she hadn't given the police. That appeared strange to me. Tess had also made a call to her brother. Now this is the second strange thing outside of not giving up all the details, her brother and his boys showed up. They were understandably pissed. Tess cried and begged them not to jump on us. She began telling her brother what happened. He took notice of Chip and Al and stared right through them. Hell, we even felt the heat, but Chip tried playing it off. Something was definitely up with those two. We gathered our items in order to prepare to check out. Tess and I needed to get to the hospital to get our wounds checked out as well. I was truly feeling every blow that connected to my body. Tess, although beaten and bruised as well, hardly showed any signs outside of her limp and her obvious bruises. Tess's brother volunteered to be our ride to the hospital. I thought it was nice of him to offer me a ride. I accepted. We cleared the room, then went and checked out, and loaded up in his car to take that trip. It was all crazy to say the least. Not a word was exchanged there nor on our way back. Unless they snuck and spoke, it was complete silence and very odd."

Mr. Hodoh wore a poker face throughout the entire story. He jotted down and asked questions periodically, but mostly listened. The clock on his wall read 4:20p.m. I knew that I needed to make sure the power was back on. I had one more run before going home and preparing for my first day back to work. Mr. Hodoh asked me to refer to him as Brayland. He also asked for any addresses or phone numbers of all individuals, even all of my bruhs. He then stood and shook my hand and stated that I would be hearing from him soon. As I walked out, I thought to contact the power company before going all the way home to check, but something told me to head home so I did.

As I pulled up in my driveway, shit felt eerie. I jumped out with my gun still on my person. I was ready to just start shooting. I was tired of walking around a nervous wreck. I have never in all my life been this messed up. This has surpassed my parent's death. I opened my door to find that my power was back up and running, which was a good sign. I walked through the house and felt a breeze coming from my bathroom. I walked backward back in the direction of the bathroom when out of nowhere Kylie appeared.

"I need to talk to you," she said calmly and with sadness in her voice. I was not hearing it.

"KYLIE for the LAST DAMN TIME GET DA FUCK OUT!"

I pulled my gun out pointing it at her. At that very moment I noticed the bruises on her face and body. She looked as though she had been beaten pretty bad recently. Although I felt her pain and had empathy for whatever happened to her, she was not my issue right now. I had no room for any more problems. She walked backward with her head down back to my door. Her hair at the top of her head was missing which meant she was snatched from the root. She finally looked up at me as she opened the door and said, "Don't ever say I did not love you enough to warn you." Kylie opened the door and left.

I walked over and plopped down on my couch and began to scream and cry. "God, what have I done? What God? Please show me what I have ever done to deserve all of this! God, I am a great friend with a big heart. I have always been an upstanding student and child. I tried never to disobey my parents. Even when they had their issues going on, I walked a chalk line. I also got great grades. Before my parent's death, I cared for each of them. I suffered depression, but this is next level bull crap. Someone or somebody's trying to drive me crazy!"

I cried and pleaded with God for what seemed like hours. I was mentally exhausted and losing it. I decided that I would go lay down early and hopefully get a jump start on some well needed rest. Oh craps, I walked down the hall and remembered my bathroom window was left ajar. I closed and locked it back. In order to have a piece of mind I decided to go through each room and check to make sure that no one or nothing had entered. I did a thorough search and decided that it wouldn't hurt to look at my video security, to see if anything was caught on my cameras that I needed to be concerned with.

Chapter Eleven

Hidden In Plain Sight

I finally had a good night's sleep without the nightmares. I felt comfortable knowing that the police had my house under surveillance at least a few hours a day. I noticed their presence on the surveillance cameras. I didn't go back far enough to know exactly when they started though. I also noticed an older gentleman sitting at the bus stop daily. Poor guy, he was wrapped up good. I hate seeing the elderly sitting alone at bus stops, it appears so dangerous to me. One day, I will go over to make sure that he is good or let him know if he needs anything he can always come knock on my door. I looked back on my cameras and watched several days' worth of tapings. I watched and looked for the time of day the police would pull up and when they would leave. The police car would be hard to detect to someone just strolling by. It also appeared strange to me the location they chose to park in. It would be impossible to surveillance my house properly from their angle. That may be how they missed Kylie at my door one day as well as leaving yesterday. After looking at the camera, I noticed that the police were definitely out there parked on both occasions. I wonder why my camera didn't catch how she got in here though. There was lost time on the camera during the power outage, I bet that is why. The camera just shows me putting her out.

She left walking in the opposite direction of the patrol car and vanished off camera. That may be the reason she didn't act up. Oh well, I am simply happy that I am being protected.

I was excited to return to work. Everyone was happy to see me back in the office. After greeting everyone, I went into my personal office to prepare for my first patient of the day. Everything went smoothly on my first day back. I was terribly busy, as I will be for the next couple of weeks. When I was off, patients rescheduled sand were scheduled in open slots for my return. I had a couple of ladies who were in their final trimester of pregnancy and were dilating, another who had warts that needed to be lasered, a few pap smears, and a couple of annual exams. I was worn out but in an effective way. It was finally time for me to pack up and head home.

I decided to stop and pick up dinner on my way home seeing that I was too tired to cook. I decided to call while en route to see what Tess was up to. I had not spoken with her in a day or so. Tess picked up on the first ring.

"Hey Tru," Tess said, smiling through the phone.

"Hello beautiful," I responded."

"How are you?" I asked her.

"I am doing okay. I am back in school and still working. I was just thinking about calling you," she said.

"You were, were you?" I questioned jokingly.

We both laughed a little before she said, "Yes."

I told her that I finally went back to work and that my first day back was great. We went on talking about a little bit of nothing until she brought Chip and Al's name back up.

"Have you seen your boys?" Tess asked me.

"No, I haven't seen them, but I spoke with Al. I have been busy doing me and focusing on my healing," was all I said back to Tess.

Tess went on talking as I went into thought not hearing too much of what she was saying. I began wondering if her brother told her that he saw all of us out and that he and Chip had gotten into it.

I picked up on her saying, "I do not know what is going on, but my brother, his goons and Chip all need to sit down before somebody gets hurt."

"I don't either and I agree," I responded. "Well, I am out picking up something to eat if you haven't eaten yet."

"I've eaten Tru, but if you want me to come to your house and feed you, I am game," she said laughingly."

"I have to work early," I explained. "But you are more than welcome to come over. I didn't invite you before because I wasn't sure if we knew each other well enough." We both laughed again before I admitted to her that I missed her.

"I miss you too, Tru."

"I will text you my address."

"Okay," Tess responded with excitement. "Give me and hour and I will be there."

"Sounds great," I said as I ended the call.

I went by The Lunch Box and ordered a family sized box of wings and a nice salad. The food is always fresh and seasoned to perfection. The owner, Envy, serves the best food in the area. Although it was still early evening, I rushed home to shower, get my clothing out for work the next day and to try and tighten up a little before Tess arrived. Just as I had that thought, I heard my doorbell, and my phone began ringing all around the same time. I let Tess in just as I picked up my phone.

"Hello." There was nothing but silence. I said, "Hello," again before I looked to see where the call was coming from. It said, private number. I hung the phone up and apologized to Tess for the interruption. I had my Bluetooth hooked up and turned it on as Uncle Charlie began singing "There Goes My Baby." We sat on the couch where I had wings, salad, and a couple of plates with a bottle of some sweet red wine sitting on the table in front of us.

We laughed and spoke more about family, friends, and our future goals. I confided in Tess that I really wanted to be exclusive, but with everything going on around us I was scared for the both of us. Tess expressed the same and opened up more about her brother Chip and Al. She began by telling me that her brother, Casper, claims he knows Chip and Al from the streets. Chip sold big time narcotics back in the day and swindled Casper out of a lot of money. Not only was Casper swindled and snitched on by Chip, but he also served time behind it. Chip served a couple of years and got out early. Chip became a federal informant and turned state's evidence against a few of the other dealers. He went into a witness protection program for a while and somehow returned to the streets on some vengeful mess. Al played a role in it all, but normally stays low-key.

"He told me to tell you to stay clear of them. They are dangerous."

"Damn," is the only word I used to begin responding to Tess. "I really don't know anything about Chip or Al from that far back and nobody speaks about it." I will definitely keep all of this in my mental rolodex and make sure I tell the investigator my new finding, I began thinking. "Well enough of all that. I want us to have a beautiful evening seeing that we haven't had much time together just enjoying one another's company."

Tess agreed as we laid back against the couch. She propped her feet up over my legs and I rubbed her legs enjoying the moment.

"I wish things could be like this all the time," I said out loud.

"Why can't it?" Tess asked.

"Tess, we just discussed this. Until all of this mess dies down, we have to be careful. Being careful at times may mean keeping our distance from one another until we find out who these people are after and why. We can FaceTime and call in between periodically sneaking and visiting like we are teenagers," I reiterated with her.

"Okay," Tess responded.

"Well, with that being said, let me give you a tour of my home."

Tess laughed and said, "Let's get to it."

I grabbed her hand and took her to the kitchen.

"This is the kitchen with all the latest amenities."

"Are you kidding me? I thought this was the bathroom," she responded back sarcastically joking.

I took Tess to every room and tried my best to kiss her in each room. There are things I like about her and things of which I am unclear. It turned into a game between us until Tess looked past me and said, "If you care so much about me, why is there a pair of women's panties on your floor next to your bed?"

I turned to look at what she referenced and was thrown for a loop. It is extremely hard to explain to someone that has trust issues that no one has been in your home. Tess broke loose from me and stormed into the living room. She grabbed her stuff and said, "I should leave."

"Tess," I said, as calm and loving as possible. "I have not entertained a woman in my home since Kylie. Trust me please, I have been honest and forthcoming with you thus far. Please give me an opportunity to figure this madness out. This has to be a setup." I am pissed off and trying to be calm because this has really gotten weird. I changed all of my locks, so Kylie has no access, yet she has gained access somehow. I am fairly sure this is a stunt of hers, but why? "Please come here, I want to show you something."

Tess walked over and we sat on the couch. She was still unsure of me, and rightfully so. I understood because I felt the same about her. I gathered my security camera and separate screen to show her my setup. I thought a little about not showing her anything and allowing her to believe what she wanted. On the other hand, I cared about her and felt that we both needed to know the truth. I rolled the camera back and showed her the two separate times Kylie came to my home. I explained to Tess that I didn't say anything because we both were already dealing with a lot. I rewound the camera too early today and slowed down the recording. Tess and I watched as Kylie got out on the passenger side of an older model car with tinted windows, not the red Altima she arrived in before. Kylie looked around and walked straight to my home. The camera picked back up on her exiting my home twenty minutes later. Kylie walked down to the car that had parked. Whomever was driving put the car in reverse and drove backward until they were out of sight. We also noticed the old man sitting there watching her enter and exit. He sat for a while before he got up and used his cane to walk away.

Tess looked at me with sincerity and apologized for doubting me. I accepted her apology, but what I did not understand, nor did Tess, was how in the hell was Kylie gaining access when the locks have been changed and all my windows were secured? Who was she working with to set me up? Tess and I stood up and went around my home checking the locks on the windows. We checked the door locks and anything we thought we could do to prevent her from coming in. While we walked around talking and producing different scenarios, Tess mentioned that Kylie looked awfully familiar to her.

"Can you remember anything about her or where you could have met?"

"No, but it's bothering me that I can't," she said.

What we did discover was a hidden camera in my bedroom. It was hidden in plain sight on the corner of my dresser. Tess snatched it off and threw it in the toilet. We both laughed and said damn at the same time. I was wondering how many more were in there, so we went in search and found one in my kitchen, one in the bathroom and one in my living room facing my security camera. It was mounted on the top of a picture I had hanging over the couch. Tess knew exactly where to look.

Just as I asked Tess if she wanted a glass of wine, her phone rang.

"Hello," she said. Tess sat looking at me with tear filled eyes. The tears began streaming down her face harder as she said, "Thank you and I will."

I reached over and hugged her wishing I could take away whatever pain she was feeling. Once she hung up the phone, I allowed her to disclose the conversation without pressing her. She sat with a faraway look in her eyes then mumbles, "This changes up everything."

I asked her what she was talking about. Tess then blurted out with anger, "My brother and a few of his partners have been shot! Somebody ran up in his house with a semi-automatic and riddled everyone in the house! According to the police, the others were pronounced dead at the scene. He was holding on and fighting to stay alive. The paramedic was transporting him to General Hospital. He was shot three times and would have gotten killed with the others if he had been in the same damn room. The police said they found my brother at the back entrance. The shooter must have caught him taking out the trash, because a trash bag was next to him. My brother always wears a bulletproof vest. I have to go be next to my brother!"

"I am going with you," I stated. I grabbed my house keys, and we locked up and left.

Chapter Twelve

The Twist and Turns

I drove as fast, yet as cautious as I could. Tess cried so hard in between praying for her brother. She took out her phone and made a call to a sister she never spoke of.

"Hello sis, oh my god Casper has been shot! Yes, he was rushed too General. I will fill you in later. Okay, I will keep you posted. Love you!" Tess hung up the line and dialed another number and waited for the person to pick up. "Hello...hello Uncle Bleep, how are you?"

"I am doing okay Tess, how are you?"

"I am not doing so well right now. I was calling to inform you, Grandma Renda, and Aunty Nellie, that Tyler is in General. Uncle Bleep, despite what you think, he was neutral. He stayed out of the way. I swear he was only trying to protect me. That's all! Now, he has been shot and may not make it! I cannot stop crying, it's my fault! Whomever it was shot up that house and everyone in it."

"Baby," her Uncle Bleep began. "I will give your aunt and grandma the message, but let me say this, this bullshit you and Casper got going on needs to stop! This game is going to get a lot more "somebodies'' killed or locked up. I have lived that dangerous life before and it is not worth it. Let me tell you another thing or two, I cannot believe y'all let that low life..."

"Thank you, Uncle! I love you."

Tess hung up the line and laid her head back just as we were pulling up to the Emergency. I was hoping that she elaborated on her phone calls. Hell, I'm still thinking about her saying her brother's house. I caught that lie. I thought it was her house, at least that is what she told me and led me to believe. Tess did mention she had family, but she never really spoke of their closeness. Either I am tripping, or her lies are exposing who she really is. Why lie to me though? All of this type of drama puts me in a bad place. I don't discuss my family period. It brings back too many bad memories that I have tucked away. On top of all that, she has never asked or even asked to meet my parents. She is aware that I have no siblings, no children or baby mama drama. That is all she needed to know anyway. Hell, we moved so fast, I am unclear of everything.

We walked in the hospital and gave them the information needed to find out the status of Tess's brother. They instructed us to take the elevator to the second floor and have a seat in the surgery waiting room. Someone would call us on the buzzer they gave us once he was out of surgery. We said, "Thank you" and did what was told. We found seats in the corner of the waiting room and sat there for what seemed like hours before we felt the buzzer going off. Tess jumped up and we headed to the reception area. They told her that her brother was in critical condition in the recovery room. They planned on moving him to the ICU and only one of us could go back to see him. We both said, "OKAY" and went back to sit and wait for the buzzer to go off again.

What seemed like another hour went by before a doctor came over this time and asked, "Are you Tess Smith."

"Yes, I am," Tess replied.

The doctor introduced himself and began explaining what was going on. "I removed one of three bullets. One was lodged in his neck centimeters away from a main artery. One was lodged in his growing and the other went straight through the left side of his head. We left the one in his neck and only removed the one from his growing, it was risky. The bullet that went through his head was clean and went straight through," the doctor explained. "For the next twenty-four to forty-eight hours things will be touch and go. You can visit with him for a couple of minutes, but he needs rest."

Tess began crying again and said, "Thank you!" She got up and walked off with the doctor to see her brother.

I took this time to call the police department to see what was taking so long for someone to contact me.

"Hello, Detective Sharpey, this is Mr. Livingston. I am calling to see what is going on with the updates?"

"My apologies Mr. Livingston, I have been meaning to call you back the day the phone hung up. I should have stopped by your home, but I didn't want to contact you or come by without concrete answers. How are you otherwise?" Detective Sharpey inquired.

"Well, it depends on what news you have for me. I have been patiently awaiting a response and have not received a call or anything one way or another."

"I understand Mr. Livingston," Detective Sharpey began. "We ran into a curveball sir. One that has caused me to contact the Internal Investigations Department. As we spoke about the day you came in. We had to hire a Digital Specialist to try developing clearer pictures from the hotel security camera. They were successful in doing so. Everything was put in evidence and tagged which is formality. I went to retrieve the evidence and brief Captain Singfield on our findings and discovered that the evidence had been removed from the evidence room." Detective Sharpey relayed, sounding defeated.

"What in the world!" I responded in shock.

"An internal investigation is being performed and someone will be contacting you," Detective Sharpey then said.

All I could say was, "Okay."

I hung up with him pissed off and feeling defeated. Next on my list of calls was Mr. Hodoh. So, I dialed him up next hoping that his news was better.

"Hello, Mr. Hodoh, this is Tru."

"Hello Tru, how is your day going so far?" Mr. Hodoh asked.

"Not good, we need a meeting ASAP sir," I stated.

"I have an opening tomorrow at 12 noon, would that be helpful?" asked Mr. Hodoh.

"Yes, I will see you then," I replied.

I hung up just as Tess came back wearing a skull on her face.

"Are you ready?" she asked me.

"Yes," I replied.

"Would you like to stay at my house tonight?" I asked Tess.

"Please and thank you. I need to get some clean clothes," Tess responded.

"Tess, I am fairly sure your house is taped off. It is an official crime scene especially since people were killed. How is your brother?" I stated.

"He is holding on," Tess responded.

"Great news. We have to continue to think positively and pray he pulls through. Baby, your brother is a fighter and so are you. If he senses that you are giving up hope, he may too. We have to believe that each day will bring forth healing. Whomever tried killing him wasn't able to do it. His life was spared. What we are about to do is go to my house and get a good night's sleep. I have to work tomorrow, so while I am at work, I want you to rest. We can visit your brother when I get off."

"Thank you, Tru but I will be at that hospital right by my brother's side all day," Tess responded with sternness and clarity. "I don't care if I have on the same clothing. I will wash them out and put them on tomorrow, which makes me any never mind! If you want, you can come up when you get off. The only thing I need for you to do is to take me by the house to pick up my truck. I will follow you back over here."

"I can do that for you baby. I have one problem though," I announced.

"What's that?" Tess asked.

"I have no clue where you live," I stated. We both burst out laughing.

"Sorry about that," Tess said while still laughing. "My mind is all over the place. The house is off of Ghent Road."

Her house my ass, I thought, she is still lying.

We jumped on the freeway and exited off Ghent Road to get to Tess's house. As we expected, yellow tape was everywhere, and the neighbors were still outside talking amongst themselves.

One neighbor spotted Tess and asked, "Are you okay?"

"Yes," Tess answered.

He began whispering and saying, "I do not know what's going on around here, but a car has been parked down the block for a couple of weeks watching your brother's house. Do not turn around! I could catch hell and be called a snitch if these nosey neighbors thought that I told anything. You seem like a nice sweet young lady," the neighbor stated.

Her brother's house was mentioned again I thought. I almost busted her out but said to myself never mind. I will bring it up later if at all.

"Thank you for that information," Tess responded.

"Could you tell us what kind of car or color?" I interrupted him and asked.

"It was a red Altima," the neighbor said.

Tess and I looked at each other and said, "Thank you again."

The neighbor walked off as I helped Tess get in her car and we both pulled off.

On my way home I was trying to put the pieces of this puzzle together. That is Tess's brother's house and not hers, so where does she live? What is she really hiding? The red Altima is the car Kylie was driving that day she came to my house. The red Altima has also been parked outside of Tess and Casper's watching them, but why? Is Chip, Al, and Kylie in on this together?

How does Kylie even know where Tess lives unless big mouth Chip or Al is involved in some form or fashion? Did Chip or Al shoot Casper or did Kylie? Are both trying to be vengeful? Where does Tess fit in? What was Kylie trying to tell me the other day? I should have listened. I wonder if it has anything to do with what is going on.

We pulled up on my block in front of my house. I had Tess pull in on the side of me. I noticed that the older gentleman was outside on the bench and wondered if I should attempt to even talk to him or not. I started in his direction and changed my mind. Tess was still sitting in her car talking on the phone. I decided to wait by her door for her to finish up her conversation so that I could eavesdrop. In the meantime, Dr. Rose's office called and said that they had an opening for 12:00 noon tomorrow. I explained to the receptionist that I couldn't take the appointment. I have another appointment for the same time slot.

The receptionist responded by saying, "Dr. Rose has your account noted. She wants to know what time would be better for you. She can adjust her schedule based on yours."

"My office is closed for half of a day on Thursday, any time after 11:30 a.m. would be good for me," I responded.

I could hear the receptionist typing my response in their system. She finally responded with, "Your message has been sent. Once she responds we will contact you. Enjoy your day."

Tess was finishing her call while opening her door. I held the door handle from the outside, being a gentleman and assisting her out. As we walked to the door, I picked up on the end of her conversation. Once we entered, I plopped down on the couch as Tess sat down next to me cuddling up under my arm. Her conversation was wrapping up. She pressed end and laid it on the table. I waited a couple of minutes to see if she would elaborate on her phone conversation, yet she said nothing.

I couldn't help myself, so I asked, "Is everything okay?"

"I am not sure. I just spoke to my sister, and she said word on the streets was that my ex-Darnell and Chip got into it earlier. They were gambling all morning and afternoon. Supposedly, Darnell shot and killed Chip over a crap game," Tess responded.

We both looked at one another puzzled. Tess looked at me and then stated, "This must mean that Chip couldn't have shot my brother and his friends."

Just as I thought this was unraveling and another twist was added. I looked at Tess and then responded, "None of this is adding up, and I am getting sick of saying it! Let me call Al. I want to see what he knows. He would know what happened seeing that Chip is his boy," I stated. "The phone went to voicemail. I will text him and hopefully he will call me back. Let me hit Derrick up."

Tess continued laying on me as I called around trying to figure out what was going on. She seemed a little tense and nervous. I looked down and noticed her hand trembling. Derrick picked up on the third ring.

"Hello, what's up Tru?"

"Man, you tell me," I responded.

"I am lost as hell!" Derrick stated.

"I feel you. This shit is crazy!" I spoke.

"I heard your girl's brother and his boys got killed. Al called and was telling me somebody ran up in Casper's house and shot everything moving. Al also told me Chip had been killed during a crap game."

"During or over?" I asked Derrick. "There is a distinct difference," I stated.

"Shit man, I have no clue. I just repeated what Al told me. He was in the vicinity when it happened. What's going on with Tess's brother? Is he going to make it?" Derrick asked. He is in ICU fighting, I responded. I am glad to hear her brother is alive. Is anybody saying anything different happened over at his house?" Derrick asked.

"No, we have no clue what went down. We just left the hospital."

"That's messed up," Derrick replied with concern and frustration in his voice. Derrick and I spoke for a few more minutes before saying our goodbyes and ending our call.

Chapter Thirteen

Destruction

"Well babe, I am exhausted. I am going to go shower and lay down. I have to rise early and need my proper rest," I said to Tess.

"Okay babe, I will come into the room as soon as I make another call."

"Okay," I responded back.

I went into my room and turned the shower on. I snuck back over to my doors opening, to eavesdrop on Tess's conversation. I need to know what the hell is going on. I heard Tess fussing at someone on the phone saying, "What in the hell is your damn problem? I do not want to hear that! Meet me in one hour!" Tess ended her call abruptly.

I snuck back in my room entering my bathroom now more curious than ever. She definitely has some involvement in all of this. But what part is my question? God, please give me a sign. Give me something concrete to stand on. I cannot be sleeping with the enemy, Amen.

I heard Tess entering and exiting my room. I was drying off and needed to brush my teeth. I heard my drawers opening and closing and wondered what the hell she was up to. Note to self, sometime tomorrow I need to go to HHG and buy inside cameras.

I opened the bathroom door quickly scaring the crap out of her. "Did you find what you were looking for?" I asked. My face was as serious as a heart attack.

"Sorry babe. I should have waited for you to come out of the bathroom. I was looking for a t-shirt or something I could sleep in. I am so sorry," Tess said.

I responded to her by saying, "No worries." Yet, I thought to myself she is about to leave, so what in the hell is she up to! I really can't trust her now. It is written all over her pretty face. Another note to self, do not invite her to spend the night ever again! What is really pissing me off is the fact that women always claim they want a good man, meet one and do grimy crap.

I found Tess a t-shirt to sleep in, even though I knew she was lying. She went in and ran bath water because she said she wanted to relax and soak. I gave her some bath beads, a towel, and a wash rag. I placed a new bath sponge on the sink as well as a new toothbrush, toothpaste, a bar of soap and liquid Dove. I politely shut the door to leave her to do what she needed. While she bathed or did whatever she was doing in there, I took that time to download face recognition on my phone just in case she tried going in my phone. I made sure all my credit cards and bank information was locked in my floor vault. I got my clothing out for work and checked her wallet to see what I could see. On her License her name is Tess E. Smith. Same with her social security card. She had no other pertinent stuff in her purse. Her phone was a little weird though. She texts a lot with someone whose name is Robert.

I heard her getting out of the bathtub, I hurriedly put her stuff back and took a seat on my bed pretending that I was looking for something in my nightstand just in case she hurried out. Once the coast was clear and she still hadn't exited the restroom, I laid back on my bed like I was asleep. I wanted to see how she was going to respond. She laid in the spot next to me, turned and kissed me, as I laid with my eyes closed not responding back. I must have drifted off because I awoke to voices coming from my bathroom. At first, I assumed I was having another nightmare, but my nightmares wouldn't allow me to respond! In my nightmares I wasn't unable to wake up. I was able to peek and hear what was going on as well as move my body with full control. I knew it was real.

"Look, do not call or text my phone! You talk too much, and you lied! My brother is fighting for his life because you decided to do things your way and not as discussed. My brother is my priority and nothing and no one else! You come near here ever again, and I am exposing you, and if need be, I will kill you myself! Play with me! I will become a big problem for you!"

I laid still, more from shock than anything. I am about ready to get up from this fake sleep and choke her out! My life is on the line, and she is part of the reason why. She has to get out right now! The problem is, I have to play my cards right. I can't let her know that I am onto the game. Once I get her out, she won't get back in. PERIOD! I have work and appointments early tomorrow; I cannot be up all night acting like a sleuth looking for clues. This chic got the game messed up. She is starting to remind me of Kylie. It is pissing me off because I told her about the games that Kylie played and how it made me feel. Although I haven't known Tess as long as I have known Kylie, she is doing the same sneaky shit. I am so darn tired, hurry up and get out I thought, as I tried to stay awake faking sleep.

"Baby, baby, wake up," I heard Tess saying as she shook me by my shoulders. I pretended a little longer just to aggravate her. "Baby, baby, please wake up," Tess repeated as I flopped back and forth as though I was trying to awake from a deep sleep.

"Yeah, what's up?" I asked her.

"I need to go up to the hospital. They called me about my brother," she lied and spoke.

"Okay, be careful." I then asked, "Do you need me to walk you out to your car?" Something told me not to wait for a response from her. I got right up and threw on some sweats as she tried to get me to lay back down. "Look babe, I wouldn't be a respectful man if I didn't get up to make sure that you made it to your car safely."

All she could do at that point was to say, "Thank you Tru."

Once Tess was ready to leave, I opened the door and walked her to her car. I instructed her to get valet parking in order to be safe. While she responded I tried looking around without it being obvious to see if I was able to see anyone outside waiting in the cut. I did not see anyone outside except for the police car doing their job. I was happy about that. I gave her a kiss and jogged back in the house. I said a prayer thanking God for the insight and jumped back in my bed. I laid back to finally relax until I couldn't remember if I put the double locks on my door. I jumped back out of bed to check the locks. Everything looked secure. I sat down on my couch for a second just to check my security cameras before I went back to my room. I watched as Tess pulled out of my driveway onto the streets. I then noticed that the police car that is usually sitting in the cut pulled out and followed behind her. That's my dog! I bet they are about to give her a tough time. Oh well, don't call me is all I thought before I put the camera down and went back to my room.

Chapter Fourteen

The Discovery

I got up early for work. Although I was tired, I knew I had to get it together and get my butt in gear. My morning went pretty smooth up until I had a thirteen-year-old patient who wanted to commit suicide. She came in nervous and clearly upset. She went against her parents' wishes, as she explained, and dated a neighborhood drug dealer. He convinced her that they were exclusive, and she was his only girl. They had unprotected sex several times. Not only was she four months pregnant, but she contracted herpes from him. She confided in me that he was seventeen years old and was homeless. What really hurt my heart was the fact that she was a teenager who made a mistake. Her mistake is life changing. She was also a straight "A" student who enjoyed school and would have to quit. She went on explaining how her parents were already struggling and could not afford to feed another child.

"Do you want me to sit down and speak to your parents with you?" I asked.

"No sir, I will do it at the right time," she responded.

She left my office crying after I gave her free scripts for her herpes medication, vitamins just in case she has to keep the baby, as well as a referral to a suicide counselor. Once she left my office, I called and reported this case. By law I had to, it was my responsibility as a professional.

I had an appointment at twelve noon with Mr. Hodoh, which I was excited about. I was on my lunch break. I finished up in the office a little early, so I headed out early. I arrived at Mr. Hodoh's office at 11:55, five minutes early. I signed in and took a seat in the reception area waiting for him to come and walk me back. The hands on the clock I continued to watch moved faster than what I wanted them to. I wanted to make sure that I was able to sit and speak about everything that has happened without having to get up and leave. My next appointment was scheduled for 2:30 p.m. I had to be back and prepared for my patient. I stood up and went to the receptionist to ask her how much longer Mr. Hodoh would be, it was now 12:15 and I needed to return to work in a timely manner. Just as the receptionist stood to see, Mr. Hodoh walked out and called my name.

"Sorry about the holdup Mr. Livingston. I had an important phone call I had to take," Mr. Hodoh explained.

"It's okay Mr. Hodoh, I actually just stood to ask if you were running behind. My time is limited as usual. I have a patient coming in that I need to make sure I am back to work on time for. I also wanted to make sure we had time to go over everything."

"I understand," Mr. Hodoh responded in sincerity. "Seeing that we are done with the formalities Mr. Livingston, what's going on?"

"I was going to ask you the same question, you tell me Mr. Hodoh."

Without saying another word, Mr. Hodoh pulled out a folder with pictures and typed notes. The first pictures he laid on his desk in front of me were of Kylie getting in and out of the red Altima. The next couple of pictures he sat in front of me were Kylie walking around the side of my house and disappearing. Minutes later she left with a guy whose body frame looked familiar, but his head was down so I couldn't see his face. The last two pictures he laid on his desk were of Tess outside my house before I told her where I even lived. She was leaning into the window of the red Altima. By now, I am boiling mad! I was so mad that my nose started bleeding from my blood pressure hitting the roof.

"Do you have any paper towels or napkins, so that I can clean myself up Mr. Hodoh?"

"Yes, sure, one second."

When Mr. Hodoh got up to get me a napkin or paper towel, my mind continued to replay this entire scenario. The madder I became, the more my nose seemed to bleed.

"Mr. Livingston, are you familiar with all the parties in the pictures I have shown you?"

"Obviously not," I answered back sarcastically. "I thought I knew the two ladies. I dated one and was seeing the other. The guy looks familiar with his body language, but I need to see his face. I have no idea who is driving that red Altima. I also want to know who the officer on duty is because they park daily and haven't arrested anybody or stopped not one damn crime! I am stressed behind all of this! It is so mind boggling, that I have begun having nightmares again," I stated.

"Well, Mr. Livingston, I have been doing some digging. The police car is not on your side, that's number one. They have been investigated and an arrest is being made within the next 24 to 48 hours. Not only your evidence, but they were tied into taking the evidence from the evidence room on several different cases. Your case opened up a can of worms. I also found out that Kylie Ellis is the long-lost mother of Tess Ellis Smith. She is also the mother of Tyler "Casper" Smith."

When Mr. Hodoh connected those dots, I almost had a serious heart attack!

"Kylie found out that Tess was back in town and Casper was out of jail from her brother Bleep. He happens to be Tess, and Casper's Uncle. Bleep has been an informant for years. We struck a deal with him that was hard for him to pass up. His information has been extremely helpful in solving a lot of cases. Especially this one. We have a few more loose ends to tie up and we will be making several arrests. FYI, the police have known for years that Chip has never told on Casper. Chip was set up. Chip and Alvin are stepbrothers. Alvin does the crimes and Chip is bated and trapped. It just so happened in this instance, he had help from the inside. Chip wanted to be accepted by his brother. Chip wasn't killed by Darnell, and nor was Casper or anyone from his crew shot by Alvin."

"What!" I yelled.

"There is more." Mr. Hodoh continued. "Chip and Kylie have had an on again, off again relationship for some time. Alvin, your "bruh," is actually engaged to Tess, but has had a side piece for a while. That same side piece set Chip up to go to jail is the same one that killed Chip, shot, and killed Casper's boys as well as shot Casper. Tess has a sister who has graduated from grad school. She is a psychotherapist and has her own practice. The sister has also reconnected with Kylie. Kylie has the one brother whose name is Bleep. She has a sister Nellie and another sister we all assumed lived out of town. Rumor had it that she cut the entire family off. It isn't true. Her name was legally changed, and she's considered more lethal than Kylie or Tess. The mighty dollar controls her, she cares less about family, not even her mother or father. Kylie's mothers name is Renda. Renda doesn't realize that she is the family trap. What Bleep doesn't find out on the streets; he gets from Renda unknowingly of course. He gives her dope, and she gives him info. Kylie's father has dementia. Mr. Smith is being taken care of by live-in-home nurses. Before I forget Mr. Livingston, the guy in the picture with his head down is your boy, Al/Alvin."

"Mr. Hodoh or Brayland, hell I don't know which you prefer being called. That is a lot of information and connecting dots. The only real questions I have left is, what do I have to do with any of their mess, and why am I the prime target? I just don't seem to understand why that dot hasn't been connected."

"We are getting closer to connecting that dot Mr. Livingston. Unfortunately, some things can't be rushed if we want to do things right. We need to make sure the information we have is solid. We are moving faster than it appeared though," Brayland responded.

"Well, I do not know if I can take it anymore. I thought that I could handle all of this, but I can't. I just can't!" I replied with frustration and anger.

"Well, Mr. Livingston," Brayland began. "You do not have much of a choice. I am working with the detective on your case, and we are on to something big here."

"How in the hell did you find out about me working with the police?" I was curious as hell.

"Mr. Livingston, I work undercover. I have been sitting in plain sight in front of your house every day. You wave at me every day. You almost blew my cover and the case a few times. It looked as though you were pondering coming over to talk to me. I sat watching them watch you, I didn't want the attention to come my way, so I would get up and leave."

"When? How? I haven't seen you," I stated.

"Mr. Livingston, I am the older gentleman with the walker at the bus stop daily."

"Holy crap!" I responded truly shocked.

Mr. Hodoh chuckled and continued, "I am working with the lead detective on your case, Detective Sharpey. He and I are a part of the same sorority. It's called Fraternity of Police or F.O.P. We met up for lunch one day to catch up on one another's lives. We began talking about work and discovered we were on the same case and the rest was history. We, as you know, ran into a little complication, but we have enough concrete evidence to put some folks away. Our issue is the same as yours, the motive. We are continuing to work as you and I speak."

"Small world," I stated.

"Yes, real small," Mr. Hodoh responded. "Anyway, if something comes up, hit me up. Here take another business card, it has my cellphone number on it. Use it if you need me," he continued.

"Mr. Hodoh, a few more questions. Was Tess lying when she said her brother bought her a home after she came out of the hospital? She claimed Darnell supposedly beat her and left her for dead? Did he even buy her that truck?"

"Mr. Livingston, yes, she was lying, and her brother did not purchase that truck. Alvin bought the house that Tess actually lives in and truck. He is also the one that installed cameras in your house. He sent Tess to your job to bate you. He never thought that she would fall in love with you and want out. Nor did she. Now her life is on the line. Chip caught on that he was being set up and went along with it because of the respect and fear he had for Alvin. Not only that, but Alvin also paid Chip a nice sum of money to take the fall and to play the role. Tess's entire family knows what is going on and they are pissed. Especially since Casper was shot."

"Mr. Hodoh, what do you suggest that I do to stay protected?"

"We still have your house under surveillance most of the day. There are times when we are not there. One of my partners comes out for a few hours when I can't. We take turns. We are prepared to call for backup if we need it. Our plan is to move in if we sense you are in danger before the warrants are issued. Try to avoid being alone with any of them, especially Tess. She is your weakness right now. Last but not least, if you have a gun, be ready to defend yourself."

"Thank you, Mr. Hodoh. I hope I will be hearing from you soon," I stated.

"You will," Mr. Hodoh responded as he walked me to the door.

On my way back to work, I remembered that I needed to stop by HHG to purchase inside cameras. I did a U-turn and went back in the direction of the mall. I found a parking spot and jogged to the door. After grabbing a cart, I went in search of a clerk who was an expert in electronics. I found a guy working on some gadgets I assumed were going on display. I explained my dilemma, and he went to the exact cameras I needed. They were easy Bluetooth installs, and I could watch from my phone. I paid at the counter and walked around to see if they sold firearms. They sold firearms and bullets. I bought two more guns and two boxes of bullets. One box had hollow points. I should have bought two boxes of hollow points. I plan to blow the scalp off of the next intruder with no remorse. I made that purchase at the front of the store and grabbed my bags heading to my car. As I stepped off the sidewalk, I caught a glimpse of a car speeding almost running me over. I moved fast as hell and watched the red Altima keep going until they got to the light and made a right. Once the right turn was made, they disappeared into traffic. I quickly jogged to my car. I sat there trying to control my breathing. I swear I almost had a heart attack!

Chapter Fifteen

Exposed

Forget all of this scary mess, now I am beginning to get pissed. They want a war; they will have a one-man war! I headed back to my office; my blood was boiling once again. I have to make a really big decision ASAP. That decision is to hire an assistant and to take some real time off work until I can get my life together, otherwise I will not have a Practice. After that, I need to find a new home and figure out how to move without anyone knowing I have moved or where. I think what I will do is find a new home, furnish, and secure it. I will use the place I am currently in as the trap house because that is what it is about to become. As I pulled up to my office, I noticed the red Altima across the street down the block a little way. I pulled up and parked anyway. When I parked and stepped out of the car, I stepped out with my head up and my chest out. I refuse to run again.

I walked in without my normal smile and went straight into my office. I checked under my desk, behind my doors, my chairs everywhere looking for cameras or a planted bug. My office felt strange, something was off. BINGO! I sat and looked straight ahead, low and behold there was a camera looking straight at me. I snatched it and stomped on it! I left my office and went to the receptionist area. I asked each receptionist and nurse if they allowed anyone in my office?

"Two ladies and a gentleman were here in the waiting area. They claimed they had an appointment. I asked for their names and was told, no need that the meeting was for pleasure, so it wouldn't be in the system with patient appointments. One of the ladies spoke up and said that they would wait, they were expecting you soon. They must have left while we were at lunch," a newly hired receptionist stated.

"Are you able to describe what they look like?" I asked.

The receptionist responded, "Yes now that you have asked, one of the ladies had two different colored eyes; they were both beautiful. The man was medium built and stood around six feet."

I thanked her and went back outside and paced the sidewalk. I had a patient to see in ten minutes and cared less at this very minute. I was up against a wall and had to get a little help. I decided to call a good friend of mine from medical school. His name is Dr. Chase Johnson.

I waited for Chase to pick up his line, I thought back on how fearless he was. Chase was a beast with a college and grad school diploma.

"He... Hello, Chase Money, what's good?"

"This has to be Tru's crazy ass. You are the only person I know who still calls me that."

"Yes, it's me," I laughingly said. "How are you?" I asked.

"I am okay. Do you remember when I told you that I was going to start my own practice? Well, I did, but it became too overwhelming. I turned around and sold the building, bought a mini trailer on wheels, and started up a mobile service. I named it "House Calls", he laughed.

"WHAT! That is awesome! Congratulations!" I was genuinely happy for him. This sounds just like something Chase would do.

"What's going on with you Tru?"

"I hate to ask you this, but man I need you. It is a lot going on here and I am losing my mind. I began having those nightmares again. Remember when I use to get them all the time? Well, this time my practice is on the line. I thought I got through the death of my parents and the nightmares. They have resurfaced. Chase Money, I need you bruh, I'm about to lose everything if I don't get my shit together."

"Man, all you had to do was say the word and I was there. When do you need me?" Chase asked.

"Like yesterday!" I responded.

Chase chuckled a little before saying, "I will be at your house by nine tonight. Just know that I am coming with some heat."

"You always do," I responded back.

Before hanging up, Chase said, "Take your meds bruh. You can fill me in when I get there."

I was happy as hell! I jogged back in the building feeling like the weight of the world had been lifted off my shoulders.

After taking care of my patients, I left work. I needed to install my inside camera and prepare myself for what was to come. I arrived home and noticed Derrick's car in my driveway. I pulled up next to him to see what was going on, he has never stopped by unannounced, so I assumed it was serious. He was laid back in his seat as though he was just chilling out.

"Hey Derrick, what's up man?" I called out as I walked over to his car.

Derrick never responded. I walked up to his window and realized that he had been shot in his head and chest. I dialed 9-1-1 and explained what had just transpired. I was leery about getting back in my car and wasn't going in the house without backup.

The police arrived in a matter of minutes and taped off my property. I watched as they collected shelling's and any other evidence and bagged it. Officers entered my home with guns drawn. They walked through each room looking for any type of evidence. Detective Sharpey and Mr. Hodoh pulled up together and joined the officers inside. Once the coast was clear, I was allowed to enter my home and speak briefly to a few officers. They asked me questions regarding my sex life, which through me for a loop, only to prepare me for what I was about to see. I was unable to enter all the way in my room. I was able to peek in while the police awaited the coroner. What I witnessed next caused me to pass out cold.

When I came to, the paramedics were asking me questions. I was a little delirious, but able to answer each. Detective Sharpey stood next to me as the paramedics continued checking my vitals. Mr. Hodoh walked over and began asking the supervising officer for updates. He headed over in our direction and was stopped by another officer and pulled in the opposite direction. I told the paramedics that I felt fine. I needed to find out what was going on. I got up and approached Mr.

Hodoh and the supervising officer's discussion. Mr. Hodoh introduced me and began explaining some of what was going on.

"Tru, are you okay?" Mr. Hodoh asked.

"Yes and no. Who were they?" Mr. Hodoh stood looking off in the distance before answering me.

"Tru, how well do you know Dr. Rose?" he asked.

"I tried making a few appointments with her, but I never got to meet her in person. Actually, I was waiting for someone from her office to confirm my appointment for tomorrow after eleven thirty. I have been so busy that I hadn't realized she hadn't had anyone call me back to confirm."

Mr. Hodoh looked at me as though he was having a brainstorm. "I see," is all he said before excusing himself and going over to speak with Detective Sharpey.

They both walked over to me and asked me to walk outside with them to get some fresh air and to allow the other detectives to do their job. We walked outside in silence and my mind began racing. All types of scenarios began playing out in my head. Right when I was about to ask Detective Sharpey for an update, his phone rang.

"Hello, yes this is him," was all he said before he said that he had to go.

Detective Sharpey took off in a light jog. He yelled back, "Mr. Hodoh meet me at the station NOW!"

Mr. Hodoh took off jogging to his car and left just like that. They both left me standing there looking confused and filled with rage. I began grabbing my head and begging someone, anyone for help! I heard myself say, "It's okay," but it wasn't okay.

"I came to help you. Put the gun down Tru." I wanted to, but I couldn't.

"Why is everybody messing with me? Why won't they leave me alone? Tell them to leave me alone!"

"Put the gun down Tru and I will make everyone leave. I promise!"

Chapter Sixteen

Go Time

"You have the right to remain silent, anything you say can and will be held against your stupid ass! Do you understand your rights?" asked Detective Sharpey. "I'm going to assume that you do, you aren't responding! Now sit your ass down before I push you down! I am handcuffing you to this table for your safety, not mines!" Detective Sharpey aggressively stated. Just as the word "mines'' exited, Detective Sharpey's mouth, in walks Mr. Hodoh.

"Finally!" Mr. Hodoh stated. "Let's start from the beginning, what is your story? "We have your boy in another room, and he has confirmed what we already know."

" I take it that you would like to continue with your fifth amendment right of shutting the hell up?" Detective Sharpey butted back in and asked."

"I would like my one phone call so that I can call my attorney please?"

"Oh, you can talk?" Detective Sharpey asked sarcastically.

"Well," Mr. Hodoh looked over at Detective Sharpey and said, "We had better get up and go find a cell phone."

"I almost lost it in there," stated Detective Sharpey. "Some people have all the audacity in the world. A damn phone is not on my priority list, we need to see if they are wrapped up over at Mr. Livingstons," he continued.

I was sitting outside a little more relaxed when I saw Detective Sharpey and Mr. Hodoh had pulled back up out in front of my house. I could tell that they were both concerned about me. Detective Sharpey assured me that this was all over. I introduced him to my boy, Dr. Chase Johnson. Mr. Hodoh said hello and asked us to give him a minute. He signaled for Detective Sharpey to come in. They both spoke to the supervising officer and stayed until everyone was gone.

Once they were satisfied that all the evidence was collected. He and Mr. Hodoh both explained that it was best to stay elsewhere anyway to clear my head and also because the crime scene was left as is. The only thing removed was the bodies and pertinent evidence.

"Okay, that's cool," I responded. Before I could ask what was really going on, Detective Sharpey said that he would like to see me down at the station by 9:00 a.m. to discuss the case. Chase and I checked into a Radisson for the week. I paid for Chace's week along with mine. It was the least I could do. We checked into our rooms which were adjoined and decided to go down to the hotel bar. We sat down there and reminisced for a few hours. When I finished filling him in, he was pissed! It was getting a little late, so we headed back to our prospective rooms agreeing to be up for breakfast at 7:00 a.m.

I could hardly sleep. I finally got up, got showered and dressed by 6:00 a.m. I sat and watched television and drank coffee until I heard from Chase. We met up, had breakfast, and headed out by 8:30 a.m.

We arrived at the police station and were greeted by Detective Sharpey. Mr. Hodoh was already seated and waiting in the office. The captain entered and took a seat at the desk. He informed Chase and I that they were running a little late. They were waiting for Internal Affairs. Small talk was made amongst the group as Chase, and I listened and said nothing. A few minutes passed and in walked a sister who walked through the doors ready for whatever. The captain asked for everyone's attention. He explained off the top that there were a lot of players in this fiasco, and he, Detective Sharpey and Mr. Hodoh would do their best to explain what was going on.

Detective Sharpey began, "According to our investigation, this is how everything played out. Your father Tru and Bleep Smith ran in the same circle back in the day. Your father made a lot of money on these streets as well as worked a nine to five. His weakness was women. Although he was married to and loved your mother dearly, he dibbled and dabbled with some of the baddest hoes in town. One night while out, he met Carlene Ellis aka Carlie Roberts. You know her by the name Officer Roberts."

My mouth dropped! I was already tripping because I had no idea that he was cheating on my mother, nor that he hustled. I sat there numb as he proceeded.

"Carlie was with your dad for years, as his main sidepiece." Detective Sharpey continued, "She became jealous and outraged when he would spend more time with your mother, than with her. Carlie gave your father an ultimatum. The ultimatum was to leave your mother or feel her wrath. Your father did not play those types of games. He was feared and respected.. He cut Carlie off and left her with nothing. Carlie was humiliated and fuming. Your dad suffered a massive heart attack and died months later. When Carlie got wind of your fathers passing, she hit the streets with vengeance. She wanted your mother gone. In her mind, she blamed you and your mother for your dad's heart attack. She was also still mad that she wasn't left any of his money. Her next mission was to kill your mother and then you. Carlie Roberts shot and killed your mother in broad daylight. She was always a suspect, but until she admitted it yesterday, we had no real proof.. Carlie was smart enough to. She was out of sight and out of mind. She made sure to disconnect and not have any contact with her family. Her brother, Bleep, kept eyes on her at all times though. When she resurfaced, she had an entirely different look. She was unrecognizable. Carlie joined the police force and continued to keep her contacts from the streets by doing illegal favors. Carlie met Les on the streets. He would purchase her for pleasure. She remembered seeing Les with you Tru when you, him and Derrick would meet up with your dad to get money. She never reminded him of this fact. They ended up staying together for a few months, until Carlie came home early and found Les with his boy Derrick in their bed." She held their downlow secret over their head.

I almost threw up! I screamed, "WHAT!"

"Mr. Livingston there is more, please let me finish," Detective Sharpey requested.

"Go on," I said.

She wanted revenge. She figured sleeping with his boy would hurt him back, so she hooked up with Alvin or Al is what the streets call him. Les nor Derrick were in any position to say anything, so they never spoke on the connection. Al was into a lot of illegal activity, long eyed and money hungry. He used her and Carlie used him and his stepbrother Chip. I suggest that we take a fifteen-minute break at this point. When we return Mr. Hodoh will pick up from here," stated Detective Sharpey.

We all walked out the door. I was like a zombie, hearing everything but unable to respond any further. My life has been a complete lie. Chase was able to guide me to a seating area. He told me to stay put while he purchased us a sandwich and a drink. He was back and sitting within five minutes due to there being no lines.

He sat looking at me for a hot second before asking, "Did you take your medication?"

I responded, "No." Chase retrieved my medication from my pockets and assisted me in taking it.

Chase also went on to say, "Look man, everything is finally coming to a head. You will be fine and able to get back to living a more normal life. You were able to do it before, this time will be different because all the skeletons will finally be out. No more haunting secrets and you will possibly be able to figure out why you have nightmares. Eat up so that we can get back in there. You got this champ. I am right here for you. Let's head back in."

I scarfed down my sandwich because I was starving, picked up my drink and got up with Chase as we walked back in.

"Everyone grab a seat so that we can continue," stated Mr. Hodoh.

We all went back to our perspective seats preparing to hear more of the discovery.

Mr. Hodoh began, "I will try to pick up where Detective Sharpey left off. Bleep contacted Carlie and Kylie informing them both of their father's health. He never told either that he contacted the other. He didn't want either to renege on coming because of the other.. They both showed up at the house and Bleep influenced them to hash out whatever differences they had on top of filling them in on their fathers health. They talked and agreed to do better. Well, they began talking more often. Carlie brought Kylie into her plan against you Tru, and hooked her up with Chip, her lover's brother. They were both as devious as the other and took pleasure in bull crapping you. Until you pissed them both off when you caught Kylie and Chip on the phone flirting. When you put her out and went after her for the money she swindled, Carlie and Kylie both promised to take every dime you had, and then kill you, but they needed a trap. Kylie kept Renda up on what was going on. Carlie knew that they needed someone just as scandalous as her and Kylie. She was determined to find someone to trap you, Tru. Carlie was preparing to leave out for work one evening and heard Chip enter the home. Al was telling Chip about a lick that he was about to hit and needed Chip to roll with him. Al had no idea that Casper was Carlie's nephew, hell she had not seen him in years herself. She thought about her conversation with Bleep. Bleep mentioned that he had bumped into him and found out Tess was coming to town. Casper was in and out of trouble most of his life. He was one of Kylie's kids. Kylie didn't even acknowledge his or either of her daughter's existence. Chip quickly agreed so they planned it out and she listened in as Al told Chip of his intentions and how much was involved. All Chip wanted to know was when and where."

Mr. Hodoh continued, "Al told him to meet him by the Rosemary Apartments where Casper hangs out in an hour. Chip said it was on and left out. Carlie left out behind them and radioed a fellow crooked officer who also patrolled that area. She gave him a head's up as to what was about to go down. She also promised him a few extra dollars to hold up on calling in for backup until she pulled up. Al saw the police hit the block. He was across the street sitting in his car eating. He called Carlie and asked her what was going on. She said, a raid. He froze for a second and asked, how much? She told him 30 bands. He asked, how about 20 along with my brother Chip and Casper? Al snitched on Casper and his brother Chip to her. She accepted the deal. Al pulled off after telling her where the money, the dope, and the meeting spot was. She hit up the money spot and let her boy and his partner get the dope, Casper, and Chip. They both stayed locked up until court. Chip was used to testify against Casper. He told a bunch of lies and the evidence although planted by Carlie, supported his rehearsed story. During the trial Carlie noticed that Tess, her niece, was there waiting in the hallway to enter the court room. Carlie told the officer guarding the door not to let her in. She was escorted out the door of the building and asked not to return. She tried calling to report her complaint but eventually gave up. Tess didn't want any attention brought to her. She was back in town and tried staying with a low profile. That was nearly impossible because of Darnell. Darnell was a ladies' man and a freak. He was also an abuser. Tess begged her Uncle Bleep not to get involved because he was sick of Darnell beating on her and planned to have him handled.

Carlie's plan was back working. She called her brother Bleep and told him since he was trying to bring back family unity, he needed to work on bringing Tess, Kylie, Casper, and the other sibling Rose together."

I looked at Chase in amazement. "They had my entire world messed up on purpose," I whispered. Chase patted my arm and refocused back on what Mr. Hodoh was saying.

"Bleep was already on to what was going on. The streets were talking and so was Renda. That is when he started giving us bits and pieces of information. Chip did a little time and was released. The evidence against him disappeared. He got time served. Casper was released not much longer afterward. This is where it gets tricky. Carlie brought Kylie to her and Al's home. Al began creeping with Kylie and fell in love with her. She didn't love him though; she loved his money and Chip. Carlie became furious, but not furious enough to mess up again. She began having threesomes with Les and Derrick to occupy her sexual thirst. Dealing with them, she needed and wanted to set things up for you, Tru, and Kylie to meet. Al was pissed but did it because of her threats and the promise of splitting your money. Chip didn't care because he was in the streets kicking it with a slew of women. If money was involved, he was down. Everything was going smoothly with you and her until you caught her and Chip slipping up and put her out, as Detective Sharpey elaborated on. Fast forward to when Tess appeared at your office. Al set that in motion with Carlie. It was said that Al took one look at her and was like DAMN! So, he played his cards right. For one, he wanted to get revenge on Carlie, and Kylie, as well as stick it to Casper. He figured fucking Kylie's daughter would sooth his wounds. Tess played along with the game and even the set up to get you, Tru. Al bought her an engagement ring, house, a truck and did practically anything she wanted him to. He even brought her sister Rose in to live with them. He paid Tess an undisclosed amount of money to be your bait. The problem came when she told him that she fell in love with you at first sight and she wanted out. Al hit Carlie up and told her about the Embassy. She paid a few thugs a few dollars to rough you and Tess up. Tess figured out that Carlie and Al was behind the hit because Rose lost one of her contacts and knew Tess knew it was her. Carlie was there in the hall. She was the one waiting at the end of the hallway. Tess began threatening to bust Carlie out to the police department if she didn't call off the hit. Carlie basically said fuck you, I will get the money and get you to do what I say one way or the other. Carlie began being posted outside your house in a police car. She became obsessed with you, Tru. She beat Kylie's ass and made her comply. Al accompanied her in the red Altima to make sure she did what was told."

"All that you have heard today was admitted to and put in writing by the suspects as well as Bleep. Bleep filled in a lot of the blanks. On top of what she admitted to verbally and in writing, she will be charged with the murders of Mrs. Livingston, Chip, and the young men that were in Casper's house. The bodies in your house, Tru, that she is being charged with are Derrick, Les, Rose, and Tess. She will also receive attempted murder charges for trying to kill Casper along with a laundry list of others that the Bureau will be handling. Carlie is looking at receiving the electric chair for her wrath. Kylie will be old and grey before she could even think to file any motions in our court system."

"This is mind boggling," I finally stated. "I am happy that this is all over! I can try to bring some normalcy back to my life."

"Well, not quite Tru, we have one more situation that needs to be handled," stated Mr. Hodoh.

"What's that?" I asked.

"Detective Sharpey, could you please let them in."

Detective Sharpey got up and opened the door.

"Bleep Smith, this is True Livingston."

I looked up and swore I saw a ghost! Chase looked from me to him and screamed, "WHAT IN THE HELL!"

We looked identical. Down to the mole above our right eyebrow. I fainted!

The End